Escape from Plum Island

D1707668

Written by Lorenzo Di Tonti

Copyright: 11/01/2021

Published: 11/01/2021

Publisher: Amazon, LLC

ISBN: 9798752686450

In 2017 I started my writing journey by writing my first novel, "Flushy: A Tale of Corporate Satire in the Insurance Industry". Flushy was a passion project for me that took over three years to write. Flushy inspired me to write a series of books within the same twisted fictional universe. Writing has always been near and dear to my heart. When I was younger, I often wrote absurd short stories that mirrored low budget Science Fiction movies. Writing has given me an avenue to control my anxiety and an outlet to produce fun stories for people to read. I enjoy sharing my brain space with other people, even if that is for a short duration of time. I don't write to write the best written books. I don't write to write epic novels. I write for fun. If you're the kind of person who reads for fun, I hope you enjoy the book.

4

Dedication

This book is dedicated to one of my oldest friends, Kevin Hodges. *One Hundred Percent* of the after-tax proceeds for this book will go to help him fight his courageous battle against brain cancer. Kevin was always there for me during my trials and tribulations and now as a show of my appreciation, I'd like to be there for him in his time of great need. If you would like to support his journey, please go visit https://www.gofundme.com/f/help-kevin-hodges-battle-brain-cancer. Thanks again for taking the time to read my book and support a great human being.

This is my second novel in a series, with the first being "**Flushy: A Tale of Corporate Satire in the Insurance Industry**". The greatest conduit for helping me learn would be writing a review online. Your candid feedback has acted as an instrumental learning tool throughout my writing journey. Whatever your experience was good, bad or ugly, please drop me some feedback.

Table of Contents

Plink! Whiz… Plink! Whiz… Whiz…. Plink!

"Slow-*it*-down, *Corporal*!", the Gunnery Sergeant shouted just loud enough to get the Corporal's attention.

The Corporal despondently released his left index finger from the trigger and rested it on the trigger guard of his *M4*. In a momentary spat of frustration the Corporal spit out a golf ball size wad of chewing tobacco.

Hwucck-poottt!

"If you shot like you spat, you'd be one hell of a marksman, son," the Gunnery Sergeant said half-jokingly.

The Corporal let out a displeasingly loud sigh and slowly tilted his head towards the Gunnery Sergeant. The glare from the sunset beamed off the Gunnery Sergeant's limited edition polarized tear drop shaped aviator sunglasses. The advice was as simple as it was frustrating, like telling an irate soon to be ex-girlfriend to 'calm down' during a ruckus shouting match. The

Corporal was hoping for something a little more insightful than, "Slow it down".

"That's easy for you to say," the Corporal replied with bated breath and a splash of sarcasm.

The Gunnery Sergeant was unphased and stood resolute over the Corporal. His arms were crossed and hands remained firmly implanted in between his armpits. The Corporal ran his fingers through his wavy blonde hair and clinched back onto the foregrip of his M4 Carbine. He squeezed the foregrip until his left hand started to turn white. The back side of his hand shined like a recently bleached toilet bowl. Sergeant D'Stefano couldn't help but smile and reiterate his advice to the young Corporal.

"Celer, Silens, Mortalis," Sergeant Tony D'Stefano said in a gingerly tone.

"Is that Latin for slow the fuck down?", Corporal Janiwosky inquired with genuine curiosity.

"Swift, Silent, Deadly. Commit it to memory. This isn't *GCE*, this is *RECON*. Every bullet counts. Reset and re-engage the target," D'Stefano suggested in a stern tone of voice.

The Corporal took a deep breath, shook off his nerves and re-adjusted the front sights of his *M4*. The shooting range was littered with spent shell casing. The range had human shaped steel targets ranging from 100 yards all the way out to 1000-yards. The backstop of the firing range was a thirty-foot tall mound of dirt and an amalgamation of 'previously-owned' military Humvee's. Firing range etiquette dictated that anything closer than 250-yards was sequestered for small arms and iron sights only. That put the nearest steel target about 250-yards down range from the two men. The Corporal slammed in a new magazine, cocked his rifle and pulled back the charging handle. The Corporal was cocked, locked and ready to roll. The feeling of slamming a new magazine into his rifle provided the Corporal with a renewed sense of tranquility. D'Stefano took a knee behind the Corporal and tapped him twice on the right shoulder. It was an affirming pat like a father reassuring his son after losing his first little league game.

"Don't just pull the trigger, squeeze the trigger. Think of your *M4* like an extension of you," D'Stefano instructed in a soft tone of voice.

The Corporal nodded his head and stared down range eagerly sighting in his target. The rifle was wafting up and down as he attempted to sight in the target. Just as he was about to stabilize the rifle, it began to drift left. He placed his left index finger on the trigger guard in a nervous attempt to steady his rifle. He took a series of deep controlled breaths and went to work. The Corporal rained led down on the target. More often than not Corporal Janiwosky hit his mark, but that still wasn't good enough for the Sergeant.

Plink! Plink! Whiz! Plink! Whiz! Plink! Whiz!

"Well, that's one way to take out a target," D'Stefano said while nodding his head up and down.

"It was the wind. I just need to compensate for the wind speed…"

"The wind? Kid, this is *Camp Lejeune*, this ain't San Diego."

Luckily for the Corporal, the shooting range was characteristically emptied out this late in the day.

Typically D'Stefano had free reign of the shooting range, everyone except for the Range Master that is. He found a sense of peace in the solitude of shooting alone.

"I think I found your problem," D'Stefano said.

"Yeah? How about you enlighten me?", the Corporal said sarcastically.

"What's her name?"

"Who?"

"*Who?* Your rifle, genius. That's *who.* What's her name?"

"What?", the Corporal answered in utter befuddlement.

"Oh, yeah. That's the problem. She doesn't have a proper name. You gotta give her a name," the Gunnery Sergeant said with a resounding tone of voice.

"You're kidding me, right?", the Corporal responded somewhat sarcastically.

"I don't joke about firearms, ever."

D'Stefano waddled over to the back of the range and

stood over a large black rifle case. He grabbed onto the case with his cartoonishly large hands and unsnapped the latches in rapid succession.

SNAP. SNAP. SNAP. SNAP.

The Gunnery Sergeant's rifle case was about Four Feet in length and covered in stickers from countries around the world. The exterior of the case resembled that of a passport of sorts for the Gunny. Some countries we publicly admitted to being in, and some that might be discovered one day through a Senate Hearing or a FOYA request.

"The sights are probably just off. I just need to make an adjustment and tinker with the scope.", the Corporal explained.

Tony scoffed at the Corporal's logical and well-reasoned response.

"Move aside, junior. Time for Betsy and I to put in some work. She ain't pretty, but hot damn is she reliable," D'Stefano said as he grabbed his 'Frankenstein' *M4* and moved into a prone shooting position. His solid-gold cross and Italian-horn jingled as he got down into his shooting position. D'Stefano adjusted the sandbags on the ground and started brushing aside all of the spent shell casings. The brass jangled like a large gust hitting a set of wind Japanese chimes.

D'Stefano stood about *Five-Feet-Five-Inches* on a good day. He was stocky as hell and had thighs the size of beer kegs. In his spare time he competed in triathlons and in his spare time strongman competitions. To prove a point, he trained his M4 on the 500-yard target further down range.

He took a deep breath and fired a controlled three-round burst. Three loud gunshots rang out like a Church Bell caught in a tornado.

Clack! Clack! Clack! Plink. Plink. Plink.

D'Stefano pulled back the charging handle and cleared his rifle. The firing range at Camp Lejeune was often serenaded with the sound of the M4 carbine. It was like music to the Gunnery Sergeants ears. No sound was quite as charming as an M4 Carbine chambered in 5.56×45mm NATO, air-cooled, gas-operated, direct impingement, magazine-fed, select fire carbine Aside

16

from the brass shell-casing falling to the ground, the range was silent. He detached the magazine and daintily placed it on the ground next to him. Smoke was still seeping out of the barrel, like the slow burn of a finely rolled Cuban cigar.

"Okay kid. So… what did I do, that you did not?", D'Stefano asked while looking back over his shoulder at Janiwosky. D'Stefano rolled over and hopped up into a squatting position. The glare from the sunlight hit his aviators and beamed a reflection back in Janiwosky's face.

"Uh... You mean aside from not being an 'Expert' level Marksman since the age of ten?", Janiwosky asked in a contumacious tone of voice.

"Kid, I'm trying to teach you something here. Don't be such a fongool," D'Stefano said in a boorish tone while towering over the Marine. D'Stefano glanced down at his Cotton Tactical Cargo pants. To his displeasure, they were covered in dust and grime. He began feverishly dusting off his pants. A miniscule mist of dust matter began to hover around the Gunnery Sergeant.

The Gunnery Sergeant discontinued the assault on his pants and took a second to 'size-up' the Corporal. Corporal Kyle Janiwosky was the spitting image, nay the textbook definition of a 'Special Operator'. Kyle stood *Six-Foot-Five-Inches*, with massive broad shoulders and a perfect V-shape physique. He had an unkempt beard, 20-inch biceps and always wore designer sunglasses. His marksmanship was suspect, but he was reliable and as tough as they come.

"I honestly have no idea…", Janiwosky replied with an inquisitive tone.

"Learn to shoot between your breaths. Take a breath, hold for a half second, shoot and then exhale. It's as simple as that," D'Stefano explained.

"Got it. In-between breaths," Janiwosky replied.

D'Stefano removed his ear protection and motioned to Janiwosky to do the same. Janiwosky reticently acquiesced by removing his 'ears' and placing them around his neck. The Gunnery Sergeant tilted his head to the side and started stroking his beard like the statue of the thinking man lost in deep contemplation.

18

"You were a machine-gunner in the *CORE*, right?", D'Stefano asked.

"Sir, yes sir. Six-Years on the *Medium,*" Janiwosky said with some spunk.

"Mhmm. What kind of equipment did they have you on exactly?"

"Nothing but the best, the M240 belt-fed gas-operated medium machine gun," Janiwosky said with a feeling of pride.

The Gunnery Sergeant started nodding his head in agreement like Sherlock Holmes stumbling upon a clue. The Gunny almost instinctively knew how to remedy this situation. The Corporal wasn't a lost cause, at least not quite yet. The Gunny was amused with the spry young Corporal. His naïve sense of wonderment reminded him a lot of how the Gunny used to be when he first enlisted.

"Yeah, that explains a lot… Okay. Here's what we're going to do. We're going to mix it up on you. Sometimes it's better to play chess, and others it's better to just flip the fucking board over," D'Stefano said.

D'Stefano walked over to Janiwosky and sized up his *M4*. Janiwosky took a lot of pride in maintaining his *M4*. He had all of the latest 'Tacti-cool' add-ons, but none of the wear-and-tear of a battle tested rifle. D'Stefano could practically see his reflection bounce off the shine of barrel.

"Ah! *There's* the problem," D'Stefano said as he snatched the Corporal's rifle.

"What? What is it now?"

D'Stefano snatched the optical scope and ripped it off the mounting rail. Janiwosky only responded with a stern look on his face, but the Gunny could tell he was triggered and teetering on losing his shit.

"*Ah.* Perfect. All-fixed. Try it now," he said and shoved the rifle into Janiwosky's chest.

Janiwosky carefully examined the rifle in a state of shock. He gingerly clasped the rifle and rotated it from one side to the other. The Corporal wasn't one to cry over spilt milk, so he went back to work. He started getting back down into his normal prone firing position. All of a sudden D'Stefano tapped him on the shoulder.

He immediately looked back at the Sergeant with a look of pure confusion.

"One more thing… Seated… Try shooting from a seated position this time," the Gunnery Sergeant said in an almost comical tone of voice.

"Seated? You're kidding me right?", the Corporal responded in a deferent tone.

"I never joke about shooting. Break up your routine. Get on your ass and put some lead down range," D'Stefano replied back in a resolute demeanor.

The Corporal wasn't amused, nor adept to change. He was however an excellent Solider. He knew when to listen. He knew when to speak. He knew when to shut up. He plopped his butt down on the ground with his legs sprawled out in front of him. He looked down range through his iron sights and focused solely on the target. He was noticeably struggling to sight in the target, the rifle was wafting in the wind. The Corporal took several long purposeful breaths and firmly gripped his rifle. Every passing breath helped the Corporal focus in on the target, like a zoom finder on a camera. He was tracking and timing his breathing, just like the Sergeant ordered. He gently squeezed the trigger followed by a loud, Plink!

"Bullseye," the Corporal whispered. There was an aroma of smugness that emboldened the Corporal. The Corporal snuck a quick smile and cleared his rifle. Smoke slowly protruded from the end of the barrel, like the last gasp of cigarette.

"Welp. That's it for today. Quit while you're ahead, that's my motto. Let's shower up and get the hell off base," D'Stefano said in a self-congratulatory manner.

"Thank god. Oh, man. There is nothing sweeter in this world than a three-day reprieve," Janiwosky cheered and slapped his knee.

The men hopped up and started packing up their weapons. The taxing nature of being a special operator weighed heavily on D'Stefano. Janiwosky picked up on the Gunnery Sergeant's mood and said, "C'mon gramps. You're making me look bad. Let's pick up the pace."

D'Stefano snapped out of his trance, scoffed and shook his head. The near two decades of service paid a substantial toll on the Gunnery Sergeant. He started packing up his gear in a slightly more intentional and expedited manner. He over-emphasized every motion and ironically stared at Janiwosky, like someone staring you down at a red light ready to race. Both men *Double-Timed* it back to the barracks.

Meanwhile at one of the bases' many in-door training facilities, Sergeant Allen found himself face down. He was pinned to the business end of a rubber floor mat. He rolled to his left and was met with resistance. He rolled to his right and was met with even more resistance. The mat was almost completely tattered and encrusted in a faded Royal Blue color. All except those worn white spider-web ripples that protruded throughout the mat. Over time the cushioning had really evaporated and the slightest amount pressure would produce a large crackling sound.

Sergeant Hernandez started laughing in between exerted breaths and asked, "That all you got?"

"I'm working on it," Allen said struggling to gain his composure on the mat. He wasn't akin to losing and didn't make a habit of giving up. In Allen's mind, it was better to lose than to give up.

"Work smarter, not harder," Hernandez murmured while rolling around.

Sergeant Allen attempted to spin out, only for Hernandez to take his back and slip into a rear-naked choke.

"C'mon, tap... Tap, sir," Hernandez said while tightening his grip.

Sergeant Allen struggled in a feeble attempt to escape the chokehold. Hernandez didn't let off the choke. He was trying to make a point. As the chokehold tightened Mike's resistance faded away.

"C'mon sir, tap! Why you gotta be so fucking stubborn all the time?"

Sergeant Allen attempted to dispute the reality of his situation and utter some kind of retort. The only audible sound he could produce was a gargled set of half utterances that loosely resembled words. The sound was reminiscent of something you would hear on the *Nature Channel*, like a Gazelle being devoured by a Boa

Constrictor. The world around him started to dissipate. The light became fleeting and his lens dampened. Just like that, it was nap time for Mike Allen.

"Sir?!?", Hernandez said with a concerned tone. To the dismay of Hernandez, the Sergeant's body was completely limp. Hernandez rolled Mike Allen over and started gently patting him on the face. Hernandez started laughing aloud to an empty room.

Allen opened his eyes and began to stare at the ceiling tiles. He was clearly dazed and confused. Hernandez couldn't refrain from laughing as the Sergeant was trying to recollect what happened.

"What's so funny?", Mike Allen said after barely regaining consciousness.

"You gotta be the most stubborn son of a bitch on this base, sir."

Mike Allen laughed off his comment in an attempt to maintain his what was left of his shattered ego.

"Opinions vary, Hernandez. I almost had you."

The mat was drenched in sweat from hours of Brazilian

Jiujitsu practice. Mike rolled back and sat cross-legged on the mat. Hernandez started instinctively stretching his legs out. Both men took a second to regain their composure and shoot the shit.

"Any plans for your leave?"

"Plans???"

"Yeah, outside of running covert warfare, I assumed you had some kind of life."

"The misses wants me to mow the yard, if you know what I mean. I just hope to get some time in front of the TV. Lite Beer, Football and family. Nothing mellows me out more than a case of ice-cold domestic piss water."

"Lite-beer, truly the sign of distinguished gentlemen. A man of refined and exquisite taste," he said with zeal.

"Not everyone used to be a corporate big-wig like you Sergeant."

"Fair enough."

"Why do you ask? What'd you got going on?" Hernandez figured Sergeant Allen was fishing for a conversation, so why not give it to him?

"I'm working on becoming an Insurance Actuary."

"Jesus Christ, why?"

"Why? Why, what?"

"Why in the fuck would you want to do that?"

"You mean, instead of sitting on my ass and drinking lite-beer and watching football?"

"Yeah? What's wrong with you? Sir."

"It's one of the oldest professions in the world."

"What is Prostitution for 500, Alex?"

"No, nimrod. Insurance Actuaries are among the oldest professions in the world."

"Yeah?"

"Yeah!"

"Okay. I'll bite. What is an insurance actuary?"

"Eh. Basically, actuaries are like odds makers, but instead of working for a crooked casino, they work for crooked insurance companies."

"Odds making, huh?"

"That about sums it up."

"Well, what do you give Detroit this weekend against New England?"

"Is Detroit playing at Home or Away?"

"I think they're..."

Mike Allen interrupted Hernandez and said, "It doesn't matter. That was a trick question. New England wins by at least 9 points. I'd bet the farm on New England for a blowout win."

Luckily for Mike Allen the "Close Quarters Combat" training facility was only 100 meters from the barracks, which made for a nice brisk stroll 'home'. On the way back to the barracks Mike noticed a small motorcade of black SUV's conspicuously parked over by the briefing room. It worried him, but not enough to inquire any further. As far as he was concerned his next mission was to take a shower and get the hell off base.

Janiwosky swung open the door to the barracks in eager anticipation to get packed up and off-base. When he opened the door the entire squad was inside unpacking gear bags. Janiwosky stood in the doorway with a confused expression painted across his enlarged Cro-Magnon brow. He started stroking his left ear lobe, clearly deep lost in thought. The rest of the squad looked up for a second at Corporal Janiwosky and then immediately went back to unpacking.

"What's so funny?", Janiwosky asked hesitantly. He slowly stepped into the barracks and started scanning the room. One thing the Corporal didn't take kindly too was being the butt of a joke.

"What so funny? You mean besides your aim, right?", Hernandez shouted from the back of the room.

D'Stefano walked into the barracks with his rifle bag slumped over his shoulder. He looked around at the squad and took off his sunglasses. He immediately read the situation and started laughing. Tony had a bellowing physicality to his laugh, he really put his whole body into it. Tony found his way to his bunk to unpack with the rest of the men.

29

"What'd I miss?", Janiwosky polled the room.

"What aside from the broadside of a barn?", Hernandez chimed in again. Hernandez was the runt of the litter in the unit, which probably accounted for his sense of humor. He never missed an opportunity to get a jibe, snide remark or dig.

"Just start unpacking new guy," Whitaker explained while neatly unpacking his seabags. Whitaker was one of the most organized operators in the unit. He had a knack for being methodical in every aspect of his life. Janiwosky looked over to Hernandez somewhat uncertain of where to draw the line. So, he poked the beehive a little.

"Hernandez… I heard stories about you," he said.

Hernandez looked up with an amused gaze at the young Corporal. Hernandez was the one normally busting balls on base and not very use to the role-reversal.

"Yeah… what've you heard?", he asked while staring daggers right into the young Corporal's eyes.

"I heard that you really put the 'special' in special

operator," he replied.

The smirk was immediately wiped off his face and his demeanor soured like a rotting banana. Hernandez was used to dishing it out, not a fan of being on receiving end of comic relief. The squad all looked up for a second at the young corporal and simultaneously burst into laughter. He sprung up ready to throw down with young Corporal. Luckily for the young corporal, Whitaker popped up and politely subdued Hernandez. Whitaker threw himself in-between the two squabbling teammates. Luckily for Whitaker, he was one scrappy SOB and none of the men dare cross him. Hernandez and Whitaker locked eyes to kick off the proverbial 'pissing' contest of the evening. Whitaker was towering over Hernandez attempting to subdue the pre-mission jitters. Hernandez grabbed the end of his mustache and wiped it with his thumb. Whitaker took both of his hands and patted him on the shoulders.

"You good, amigo?"

Hernandez smiled and nodded at the Sergeant like a cowboy tipping his hat. It wasn't the first time some new guy tried to pull some macho bullshit. Whitaker felt that

31

with that kind of attitude the Corporal would fit right in with the rest of the men.

"I'm good, buddy. I'm good. These fucking new guys, man."

Whitaker had fourteen distinctive and equidistant thick black lines tattooed on the inside of left forearm. One for each of the EOD technicians who perished in Iraq and Afghanistan since 2005. He made a point to keep his sleeve perpetually rolled up as a sobering reminder of the courage and sacrifice it takes to be an EOD Technician. Whitaker spent his first two tours of duty cutting his teeth in the Explosive Ordinance Disposal (EOD) unit during the height of operation Al Fajr. Whitaker often found himself playing 'Dad' within the Camp. Every family has issues and for the Marine Recon regiment at Camp Lejeune that's exactly what it was, a family.

"Nice to meet you by the way. I'm Whitaker, callsign 'Tortuga'," Whitaker replied and stuck out his hand to Janiwosky. Janiwosky eagerly obliged, he wanted to make a good impression with the rest of the squad. He sure did have a funny way of showing it.

"What's the deal? Their shipping us out? Where to?", Janiwosky briefly protested to the group. The men picked up on his nervousness. It was only customary for the new guy to have a bit of unease going into the first mission briefing.

"Preach, what do you make of all this?", Hernandez asked his devout teammate. Hernandez weakly protested the situation by shoving his bags under his bunk, like a teenager begrudgingly doing laundry for the first time.

"And you will hear of wars and rumors of wars. See that you are not alarmed, for this must take place, but the end is not yet. For nation will rise against nation, and kingdom against kingdom, and there will be famines and earthquakes in various places... Matthew," Preach opined in a stoic tone as he read passages from his handy pocket Bible. It was an old pocket Bible that Lindell kept tucked away in his boot.

"Good shit, Preach. Good shit," Hernandez said.

"Real fucking ominous, as always," Barnes said under his breath. The years of attending to dying comrades hardened Barnes in a way that made him rather cynical about war. The way he figured it, he could be part of the problem or part of the solution. He found solace in serving as a Medical Corpsman. Barnes wiped the melancholic look from his brow and made his way over to the briefing room without so much as an introduction to the new guy. Without notice Preach sprang up and stuck his hand out to introduce himself to Janiwosky. Preach stood Six-Foot-Seven-inches tall and weighed in at a lean about 225 pounds. He was a slender mountain of a man, with a soft spoken yet rusty tone of voice.

"Corporal Lindell Jones. They call me Preach. Nice to meet you kid," the Corporal said in a deepen tone of voice. Lindell was covered shoulders to feet in tattoos. He spent his formative years on the streets of South Central. Lindell had that leathered street skin, the kind of thick skin acquired from hundreds of street fights and unfortunate run-ins with the wrong side of the law. After too many near death encounters, he chose a higher path, the righteous path. Lindell devoted his life to his God and to the Core. Janiwosky quickly shook hands with the Corporal and went back to aimlessly wandering the barracks.

"You can gripe till the cows come home kid. That ain't

gonna change the fact our reprieve is DOA. One piece of advice, just don't be late for the briefing kid," Corporal Barnes squawked. Barnes was sifting through his foot locker searching for something. Barnes had one of the most unkempt bunks, but nonetheless the men entrusted their lives with him. Janiwosky accepted the advice with a nod and a wink. Janiwosky pulled D'Stefano aside for a brief consultation.

"What's the deal with Barnes?", he whispered as silently as a librarian.

"The deal? Don't mind Barnes. His bedside manner is a lot like his foreplay, in that it's extremely brief and lacking of tenderness," D'Stefano replied.

"Oh. Okay."

"Yeah, don't take it personally. Why do you think he's callsign is 'Zippo'? He's quick and useful in a pinch."

Janiwosky started navigating his way towards his bunk. He traversed carefully through the labyrinth of bunks and seabags. He made sure not to disturb any of the luggage left behind by his fellow crewmen. As soon as he was able to manage putting his bag down, Mike Allen stepped into the foreground of the room with a commanding presence.

"Nice to meet you kid. I'll see you at the brief," Lance Corporal Yamada said while patting him on the shoulder. Yamada was short and slender. He had slicked back razor black hair with a tattoo on his neck of Aces and Eights. Yamada was one of the new transfers from the Raider regiment. He was quiet and reclusive, but the men appreciated his resolve.

"Drop what you're doing. Let's double-time it to the mission brief," First Sergeant Allen shouted to the remainder of the squadron.

One by one they disembarked from the barracks and expeditiously headed over to the briefing room.

"Yo, Tony! Where do you think we're shipping out to this time?", Mike Allen asked his comrade in arms.

"Mike, that's above my pay grade buddy," Tony replied.

The briefing room was a chock-full of colorful chit-chat and teeming with the generic military banter. Mike found a comfortable sense of enjoyment in the predictability of it all. For Mike, his life in the Marines was all rather straightforward. The Detachment Commander gave orders and Mike followed them out to the letter. The briefing room was poorly lit and stunk from the aftermath of diets chalk full of excessive protein shakes. Nothing quite compared to the distinctive odor of a heavy discharge of fecal matter topped off with *Whey Protein*. The Department of Defense really spared no expense when designing this part of the base. Mike often noted how unlike other briefing rooms this briefing room had its own wall mounted air conditioner. The floor was an old commercial grade carpet, which was rarely if ever cleaned.

Tony stealthily stretched out his arms in order to scope out the room for some clues. He looked to his right. He looked to his left. He looked up at the ceiling and slowly rolled his head backwards and looked behind him. To D'Stefano's surprise, there were a number of new faces sitting around the room. Tony couldn't help but wonder who they were or more importantly why they were attending the briefing. Aside from the notable absence of the *Assistant Detachment Commander*, nothing else struck him as too out of the ordinary. Tony and Mike tended to sit in the back of the room to get best vantage point. That way they could always see who showed up late for the meeting. Both men placed a tremendous amount of value on punctuality.

Tony nudged his head over to Mike and pointed over at the newbies up in the front row. Mike just shrugged his shoulders and pulled out a pack of cigarettes from his front pocket. Mike started tamping down on the pack of cigarettes against his palm. He pulled out a loose cigarette and offered one up to his partner in crime. Tony immediately obliged and grabbed the 'loosey' out of the pack. Mike picked up his smoking habit out of pure convenience. See in the Military smokers get two extra

10-minute smoke breaks per day. Which means over the course of twenty years of service Mike would get an additional One Hundred- and One-days' worth of smoke breaks. The way Mike looked at it, you'd be stupid not to smoke.

"Thanks bud," Tony said.

"The way I figure it. If I don't look out for you. Who in the hell will?", Mike said sarcastically while handing his buddy a 'cancer stick'.

Mike Allen wasn't the most foreboding or physically intimidating soldiers. He stood 5'11 on a good day with olive oil skin and a luscious full set of slicked back brown hair. He weighed in about 170 pounds soaking wet. He wasn't the most distinguished solider, but was adept to making friends in high places. He always found it important to make people feel important. Tony and Mike had an unshakable bond, the kind of bond that is built on heritage. Back in the day they're great grandparents came over on a boat from the same part of Italy. Just as Tony was about to say something to Mike, the room was spurred into complete silence. The Detachment Commander, Commander Russel, muscled his way into the room and made a B-line to the front of the briefing room.

First Sergeant Mike Allen immediately noticed, hopped up and shouted commandingly, "Officer on deck! Ten-hut!"

Everyone in the room jolted up out of their seats and stood at attention saluting the Detachment Commander. It was a rare occasion for the *RECON* unit stationed at Marine Corps Base Camp Lejeune to get a debrief from the '*Top Brass*'. This clearly wasn't a *run-of-the-mill* mission briefing. Mike and Tony did a double take and looked at each other in blissful amazement. For Mike this meant some quality time for brown-nosing and for Tony it meant the men we're fixing to get in a good fight.

"At ease, *Men*," the Commander said in a silvery-sultry tone. The kind of tone that is earned through the crucible of *Three-Decades* of Military service. The Commander waved us off and pointed at the projector with one of those cool wireless projector controls. His uniform was congested with decades of distinguished 'chest-candy', though these days some of the medals had started to lose

41

their luster. The mantle of leadership weighed a noticeably heavy burden on the Commander. During his tenure he was witness to countless Marines being killed in action. Every mission carried its set of risks and the men were all well aware that this mission, like the one before it, could be their last.

"Gentlemen, this morning we had an incident on Plum Island.", the Detachment Commander said sparingly.

The Commander wasn't much for beating around the bush. He stood *Six-Foot Two Inches*, shoulders back, chest out and donned the typical $5 Officer's Crewcut. His hair was a salt & pepper silver, without a speck of facial hair on his newly polished chin. The Commander was a stickler for facial hair. He made a point to periodically call out disheveled beards or overgrown mustaches. On an average Saturday morning he could be found at the base Barbershop getting a straight-razor shave and hot towel service.

"What happened? Did another Montauk Monster wash up to shore?", Hernandez asked.

Staff Sergeant Miller smacked *Sergeant* Hernandez on

the back of the head, like a father scolding his son for cursing at the dinner table. The men all respected the hell out of Staff Sergeant Miller. For the Staff Sergeant, Soldiering was a rite of passage in his family handed down from generation to generation. He was young dumb and full of... well, you know how it goes.

Hernandez was regularly placed at the front of the 'class'. Mostly as an example for the other crewmen as to 'How *not* to Act'. Hernandez tended to filter the grim reality of *War* through the lens of humor. He was the class clown, every unit has a wise ass, every unit has a 'Hernandez'. Luckily for Hernandez, he had a talent for resurrecting bad situations and was one hell of a Gunner.

The Commander despairingly shook his head and continued the brief, "A downed ship washed ashore onto Plum Island at or around *Zero-Nine-Hundred Hours*. Aboard that vessel an unknown number of survivors were rescued by Plum Island Security. The Coast Guard sent in a rescue chopper that responded to the scene of the crash at approximately *Ten-Hundred Hours*. From what we can tell, the Coast Guard rescue effort failed and neither the Coast Guard nor Facility staff on Plum Island have been reachable. All communications in or

43

out of the island are inoperable."

"So, what happened?", Staff Sergeant Miller questioned.

"Unknown at this time," the Commander responded quickly.

"What's the current state of the island?"

"Unknown at this time," the Commander responded sharply.

"What about the Island personnel?", Hernandez asked.

"On a normal day, Plum Island has approximately 400 employees working throughout the facility. The island operates on a skeleton crew over the weekend. We estimate there are approximately three dozen employees on the island. All of which whereabouts are currently unknown," the Commander explained.

"What about the Platoon stationed at Fort Terry?", Tony D'Stefano asked.

"Unknown at this time. We can only assume they're assisting the island personnel secure the facility or aiding in the restoration of critical infrastructure," the

Commander replied.

Mike leaned forward just as someone from the front row abruptly stood up with a stack of Mission Dossiers in hand. He wasn't military, Mike and Tony figured he was probably a 'Company Man'. He had aviators on, a pin-striped black-suit and a Five O'clock shadow a yard long. The men assumed he was with the CIA and collectively felt an uneasy mood wafting around the room.

Mike whispered to Tony, "*C.I.A.* Who else in their right mind would wear sunglasses indoors?"

Tony whispered back with his hand covering his mouth, "What an asshole…"

The suit started walking around the room handing out the Mission Dossiers to the team members. He dropped the Dossiers like a spoiled rich kid casually dropping Benjamins at a strip club.

"In front of each of you is the Mission dossier. I suggest you commit it to memory before we get airborne," the Commander said.

The Commander took a brief respite and stood at the front of the room with his hands crossed behind his back. He scrunched his eyebrows up. The men could tell he was adrift in thought. The Commander was a very transparent person by his very nature. He wore his feelings on his sleeve and his attitude on his face.

"Operation "*Tag Team*"? Did the boys over at the C.I.A. run out of names or something?", Hernandez asked loud enough for the entire room to hear.

Staff Sergeant Miller pulled Hernandez in close and whispered, "Hernandez... *shut-the-fuck-up*! Or I will have you cleaning the latrines for the next six-weeks."

The Commander took a big sigh and continued the brief, "I'm glad you can read Sergeant Hernandez. That will come in handy where you're going. On its face, Plum Island is a top of the line "*Animal Disease Center*". In reality, this is a United States biological warfare research laboratory, a BSL-4 Bio Weapons Lab. This is a joint Marine RECON/Coast Guard rescue operation. So, try not make the Coasties look bad in the process. For all intents and purposes this mission is going to be couched as a Special Reconnaissance exercise."

The Commander slowly pulled a cigar out of his right chest pocket. He took a second to light up the cigar and slowly began to puff on it. He took the cigar out of his mouth and blew a smoke ring, or at least attempted to blow a smoke ring. In reality, it was more like a dilapidated oval. Mike and Tony both lit up their respective cigarettes.

"Your mission is to re-establish communication with the island personnel and figure out what in God's green earth is happening on Plum Island. This could be anything from a botched terrorist attack to a rolling power outage or anything in-between. Hell, this could be as simple as a blown fuse box for all we know. In all reality, the Coasties probably just couldn't figure out how to flip a circuit breaker back on."

The room laughed out loud, all except one man leaning up against the back wall. Mike nudged Tony with his elbow and subtly pointed over to the foreboding figure in the corner of the room. Tony had no clue and just put his hands up in confusion. For all Mike and Tony knew, he was another CIA goon sent to baby sit the Marines.

"Do we have any intel on the ground? Anything at all?",

Staff Sergeant Miller asked.

"Negative," the Commander affirmatively replied.

"Are we expecting any resistance sir?", First Sergeant Mike Allen asked.

"From who? The Coasties? The Fisherman? The scientists? Yeah… expect a lot of resistance," the Commander responded sarcastically.

Everyone laughed out loud, again. One thing Mike learned long ago, was that during mission planning, there were no stupid questions. The mood was relatively tame given the circumstances of the op. This was more or less a glorified training op.

"No, we're not expecting hostile resistance. Sweat saves blood gentlemen, blood saves lives and brains save both. For all the new people in the room. This is a perfect chance to get your feet wet operating in one of the most dangerous environments known to man. Plum Island is one of the most volatile Bio-Labs in the world. Tonight, you could be going up against the most dangerous enemy. You could be going up against the invisible enemy," the Commander said.

"What about the *UAV*? Did it pick up anything?", Staff Sergeant Miller asked.

"As far as we can tell, from the air, the island has gone completely dark. Heat signatures seem to be minimal and activity on the island appears dormant from above. That's not *too* unusual considering the local weather patterns and the majority, if not all the staff would be indoors in a storm like this. Here's the bad news. The bad news is, there is a possibility of a chemical outbreak on the island, so be prepared to stop often for periodic contamination checks," the Commander said.

"Great. So, we're going in blind, deaf and dumb," Hernandez said.

"Check that bullshit, Hernandez," Staff Sergeant Miller said.

"Sir, yes sir," Hernandez said as he plunged his hands into his pockets.

"Sir, why don't we just wait for the power to come back online? Why are we sending in a Special Ops Team for a power outage?", Tony D'Stefano asked while puffing down on his cigarette.

"The Bio Weapons Lab is designated as a High Value Target and operates in a negative pressure environment," the Commander explained in a condescending tone.

"Negative pressure?", Mike replied completely bewildered by the explanation. Mike had little more than a high schools worth of biology under his belt.

"Lieutenant Colonel Johnson, this might be a good time to step in to the conversation," the Commander said while gesturing to the mysterious man.

The Commander pointed at someone in the front row, presumably the Lieutenant Colonel. One of the gentlemen in the front row stood up and turned towards the men. His hands firmly affixed to his hips and an unlit cigar sticking out of the side of his mouth. He chewed on the cigar without lighting it up.

"Viruses have to be kept in a negative pressure environment at all times, otherwise they could simply float off into the atmosphere. In theory, the back-up generators should have kicked in by now. Thermal scans of the island show no such luck. The island had a similar power failure back in '02, which led to some minor contamination seepage. Let's pray that's the case here and nothing more nefarious is a foot. The longer we wait gentlemen, the worse outcome we can expect," Lieutenant Colonel Johnson explained.

"Lieutenant Colonel Johnson is on loan from the Department of Defense, he is retired a Bio-Chemical Weapons Specialist for the DOD and will keep you from blowing up the island and or accidentally unleashing the next *'Spanish Flu'* on mainland America. He was the point person between the DOD, MARSOC, NIH and the CDC. Prior to his departure from *MARSOC* and subsequent retirement from the CORE, he was the acting Commander of Fort Terry. His knowledge of the Island, the infrastructure and Bioweapons is crucial to mission success. For all intents and purposes, the Lieutenant is acting as Intelligence Sergeant for this mission," the Commander explained to the Marines.

The Commander took a long puff of his cigar and placed his arms behind his back. He snapped his head side to side like someone who was trying to get sea water out of their ears. His neck made an audible cracking sound.

"We're going to assume the worst-case scenario, a

power failure which led to a viral outbreak. Gentlemen, best-case scenario is that the power just failed and everyone is following a strict quarantine protocol. What better time for a high-risk scenario training op?", the Commander explained.

Tony D'Stefano raised his hand and sheepishly asked, "Sir. What kind of viruses are we talking about here?"

The man in the black suit finally found an opportune time to interject himself back into the conversation. Without flinching or budging an inch he said, "The kind of viruses that are above your pay grade sailor. *That kind.*"

"No offense. But, who the fuck is this guy?", Tony asked.

"Sergeant... D'Stefano, is it? I'm not familiar where you earned your PHD in Micro Biology and Chemistry. Did you write a 1,000-page dissertation on the Epidemiological and Molecular Approaches to Study the Transmission and Treatment of Lime Disease? *That-is-who-the-fuck-I-am,*" the man said in a reticent tone of voice.

The room was drenched in an uncomfortable air silence. It was becoming abundantly clear that this mission did not sit well with the men. The projector started to get obscured by the lingering cigar smoke. The Commander took a long dramatic pause followed by another plume of cigar smoke. He smiled with the cigar in his mouth. His teeth were almost a florescent white. For all intents and purposes the Commander took pride in his appearance.

"Okay. Let's get the logistics out of the way. Hernandez is running Comms, Barnes you're on Medical, D'Stefano… Weapons Sergeant, Whitaker, Engineering. Let's put this package together and wrap a bow around it," Commander said.

The Commander put up a map of the Island and said, "Whitaker, you're up. Target Analysis."

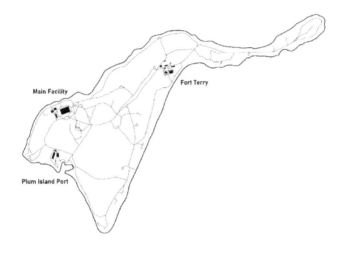

Todd Whitaker slowly rose up from his chair, walked
over to the projector screen and began inspecting the
map. Whitaker slowly pulled out his reading glasses and
snugly pressed them up against his face. His reading
glasses had cartoonishly large opal shaped lenses and a
thick black plastic frame. The light of the projector was
dampened by the amalgamation of cigar plumes and
humidity.

"The island is only two miles to the mainland, but the weather and surrounding rocks would make a beach incursion untenable… So, CRRC boats are completely out of the question," he explained while pointing to the map with a half-cocked index finger.

He started looking over the mission dossier and said, "Since we have *zero* intel on the approximate size of the resistance, or if any resistance exists, I'd say the island would be most vulnerable to an aerial incursion 1-click west of Fort Terry. It would be reasonable to assume that the target of an invasion would be the Biolab and not the Fort."

Whitaker started chewing on the end of a cheap plastic pen. He took it out of his mouth and started scratching his head with it. After about a minute or so of fidgeting with the pen he stuck it back in his pocket. The pen started bleeding into his BDU and made a large swell of blue ink on his chest. Whitaker was unfazed or unaware of the ink blot forming on his chest. For someone so smart, the men thought he sure acted pretty stupid from time to time.

"A possible secondary landing zone could be the rooftop

the Main facility, *Building 257*. That's our ideal point of accessibility for infiltration and maybe even *Ex-fil*. Assuming there is no 'real' resistance to speak of," Whitaker said.

"One squad deploys on the back side of the island and one squad repels onto the rooftop of the main facility. Everyone agree with Sergeant Whitakers assessment?", the Commander asked.

"Ho-rah!", the group chanted in sequence.

"Land on the roof? Why not just knock on the front door and invite ourselves in for tea and crumpets?", Hernandez said under his breath.

Todd started aggressively stroking his beard and said, "Now, the immediate problem is turning the power back on…"

Lieutenant Colonel Johnson stepped in and volunteered some useful information to the group.

"There's an independent nuclear reactor on the Island and a series of redundant diesel-powered back-up generators just outside the main building, building 257.

The reactor is housed on sub-basement level 5," he said.

"The building goes down five stories? On an island?",
Todd asked somewhat perplexed by the obvious design
flaw.

"Well, yeah. I mean, the building was designed to
collapse in on itself. We're talking about the deadliest
viruses known to man. What better failsafe to contain the
apocalypse? There are four floors below the surface of
the Island, all of which contain experimental Bio
Weapons and genetically altered diseases. The deeper
you go, the more apocalyptic the virus. That is aside
from sub-basement 5, which purely is there to house the
nuclear reactor," Johnson explained.

"Collapse in on itself? Oh, yeah. That sounds just
lovely," Hernandez murmured. He was followed by an
encore of confused outbursts and objections. The
Detachment Commander simmered in the consternation
of the two squads, he relished in the schadenfreude. The
way he figured it Special Operations was about high-
level strategic military problem-solving. If it were easy,
then anyone could do it.

"Got it. Uh-huh. So, I think the easiest plan is to get the generators back online."

"Don't worry about the generators."

"Don't worry about the generators? Excuse me, sir. My job is to worry, plan and execute."

"Son, if the generators aren't on, they ain't working,"

"Yeah, but what if--,"

Erh-unnnh

The Detachment Commander interrupted the Sergeant by overtly clearing his throat. Whitaker wasn't fond of semantics or reading between the lines. Whitaker wasn't fond of getting publicly reprimanded either. Whitaker looked over at the Commander and took that as a sign to move on.

"*Okay*. I guess the real question is, how do we get access to the reactor?", Todd asked.

"Sub-basement 5 has two possible access points. There's a private elevator exclusively designed to access sub-basement 5. Sub-basement 5 can also be accessed through the main stairwell," Lieutenant Colonel Johnson said.

"Talk to me about the main stairwell," Whitaker inquired.

"Unlike the elevator, the stairwell requires us to sequentially breach each floor to access a lower level. Another failsafe when the power goes down," Lieutenant Colonel Johnson explained.

"Okay. Yeah, fuck that noise. Instead of traversing a maze of individual Bio Weapon Labs, how do we access the elevator shaft?", Whitaker asked.

Whitaker stood there and invited the Intelligence Sergeant to provide some very much needed intelligence. Lieutenant Colonel Johnson said nothing and deferred to the Detachment Commander for an answer.

"Dr. Lisa Kerrigan is your point of contact for the facility. She handles oversight of the entire facility operations on the Island. Finding Dr. Kerrigan is mission critical. She holds the keys to the kingdom, so to speak. You're to find her and figure out what in the hell happened. Get the island back to operational status ASAP. Find the Coasties and the fisherman, then you get the hell on out of there. Am I clear?", the Commander explained.

"Sir, yes sir!", the team said in unison.

"Weapons Sergeant. Front and center. You're up," the Commander said while scanning the room.

Tony D'Stefano sprang up out of his chair and stood at attention at the front of the room. He started looking over the Mission Dossier and rubbing his right arm. He took a deep sigh of relief and explained, "We need to play this one by the numbers. We need a fuck-up-proof load out. At minimum we need one *High Volume Aerodynamic Particle Sizer* per squadron, *Level A Hazmat Suits*... Unfortunately for us, shotguns and any explosive ordinances are completely out the window," Tony explained.

"What about breaching charges?", Staff Sergeant Miller asked.

"What about them?", Tony questioned the Staff Sergeant.

"How do you plan on breaching the facility? If the power is off, the facility automatically locks down tighter than a pastor's daughter on prom night," Staff Sergeant Miller replied.

D'Stefano looked over at Lieutenant Colonel Johnson for some kind of guidance. For an intelligence officer, Johnson wasn't providing a heck of a lot of intelligence.

"How'd you people manage to breach before explosives? Back in my day we used nothing more than axel grease and torque."

"Right... In that case, each man will be equipped with a new toy courteous from our friends over at DARPA. It's a standard *M4 Carbine*, chambered in 5.56×45mm NATO, but with a special twist. This M4 has a special Boron Coated barrel, making it weather proof and prevents jamming. Each squad needs a sledge hammer, two wrecking bars and a hydraulic-extrication rescue tool, which I assume we can borrow from the Coasties. Each man needs a regulator, spare oxygen tank and plenty of duct tape," Tony explained.

He took a second to inconspicuously adjust his bulge

from the right side of his pants to the left.

"I mean, aside from our standard gear kit, that's about all I can think of," he explained.

"Everyone agree with D'Stefano's assessment?", the Commander asked.

"Hoo-rah!", the group said in unison.

"Medical Sergeant, front and center."

Barnes sprang up out of his chair and walked to the front of the room with his mission dossier in hand. Barnes was attempting to quit a pack a day habit he earned during Operation Iraqi Freedom.

"If this mission goes Direct Action, which let's assume it does for the sake of planning..."

"Safe assumption," the Intelligence Sergeant interrupted.

"I want each man equipped with an *Automatic Distress Signal Unit*, plenty of Morphine, Adrenaline, Atropine and a hear rate monitor."

The Intelligence Sergeant gave his nod of approval to the Commander like a catcher calling out signs to a relief pitcher.

"Consider it done," the Commander said with ease.

"It is *Seventeen Fifty*. We have *Thirty-Minutes* to get mission ready and mount up. We are wheels up at 18:20, we take a *Chinook* from Camp Lejeune to link up with the Coast Guard transport off the coast of Plum Island. The Coast Guard was nice enough to lend us two Black Hawk helicopters for the trip over. Each Team will encircle the island for an aerial Search and Rescue. If there are no visible signs of distress, which is probably the case. Alpha Team, which will be led by Sergeant Allen, will deploy on the backside of the Island at no later than 20:00. Alpha Team will approach the island from the East and Bravo Team from above. The drop zone will be directly adjacent to Fort Terry, which from what we can tell is completely deserted. Alpha Team will be flown in by Coast Guard Commander Riley, his call sign for the mission is *Red Sparrow*."

The Commander took another big puff of smoke from his bottom shelf cigar. He'd nearly gone through that entire cigar in near record time.

"Don't worry, he's one of the best pilots the Coast Guard has to offer. After checking-in with the troops at Fort Terry, Alpha Team will make your way to the Weapons Lab and link up with Bravo Team. Alpha Team will be designated as the Assault team and Bravo Team will provide overwatch. Bravo Team will be flown in by Commander Hodges, call sign *Silver Spoon*. If there is no resistance, which is likely the case, you should hit the Bio Lab by no later than *Twenty-One Hundred Hours*."

"Sir. What's the abort plan?", Hernandez asked sheepishly.

"Well, the Island is two miles from mainland USA. So, if shit hits the fan. Just swim for it," the Commander said sarcastically.

The Commander's words were immediately followed by a chorus of cachinnation from the operators.

"Hernandez this is a rescue op with zero signs of hostile resistance. Why in the fuck would we need to abort? I mean, we're better off bringing monkey wrenches, rather than bullets on this mission. Consider it a vacation

64

compared to the shit we normally face off against," Tony D'Stefano scolded Hernandez.

Tony's patience was worn razor thin by Hernandez's refractory attitude. Once the laughter subsided, the Commander stepped back in to wrap up the mission brief.

"Bravo Team, which will be led by Staff Sergeant Miller. Bravo Team will rappel directly from the Blackhawk onto the rooftop of the main facility. Bravo Team will secure the primary objective and cover Alpha's approach as they sweep the island for any hostile elements. Once both teams link up at the main Weapons Lab, approximately at 21:30, you will simultaneously hit the target. One team from above, and one from below. Try to play nice with the Coast Guard when you get there. Best-case scenario they open the front doors with open arms and we all make it back to base in time for Margaritas by *24:00*."

"Hoo-ra!", the group shouted.

"Any questions?", the Commander asked the room.

"No Sir!", the group shouted.

"You have your orders. Let's go do what we do best, men."

"Aten hut!", D'Stefano commanded the squadron.

Each man stood at the ready on the sodden tarmac. Mike Allen walked up and down the line of battle-hardened operators. He inspected the team with a fiery anxiety. This was his first mainland mission as Team Leader and by the vigor he chewed his tobacco, he was determined to do it by the book.

"The Coast Guard spared no expense on the transport," Mike Allen said sarcastically pointing to the sturdy, but reliable *UH-60* Black Hawk helicopters supplied by the Coast Guard.

The team laughed and popped off some pre-mission one-liners. None of the men had actually trained for this specific scenario. The brief commentary was muddled by the rain and the backdrop of the Black Hawk's spinning up for lift off. The blades of a Black Hawk made a distinctive sound spinning in the rain.

Whum. Whum. Whum. Whum.

"We're gonna do this one by the book, gentlemen. We're the *Ghosts in the Darkness*. We're the tip of the fucking spear. We're the best of the best. We are Recon. Slow is fast. Fast is smooth. Watch your fields of fire and don't pull that trigger unless you are 100% certain…", Allen said singling out Corporal Janiwosky by punching him in the chest.

"Hoo-rah!", the group shouted.

"Preach. Front and center. Let's kick this part off right," the Sergeant shouted in the rain.

Corporal Lindell hustled to the front of the line. Sergeant Allen took a knee, which cued the squad to follow in kind. Each man slung their rifle and took a knee. All except Lieutenant Colonel Johnson who stubbornly stood at attention. Preach pulled the bible from his boot and held up his hand over the men.

"And I saw the beast, and the kings of the earth, and their armies, gathered together to make war against him that sat on the horse, and against his army. And the beast was taken, and with him the false prophet that wrought miracles before him, with which he deceived

69

them that had received the mark of the beast, and them
that worshipped his image. These both were cast alive
into a lake of fire burning with brimstone."

Corporal Lindell slammed closed his bible and stuck it back into his left boot. He had an uneasy feeling about this mission and wore the burden of nervousness like a cheap suit on a private Detective. Mike wasn't a religious man, but the verses helped convince the men to be brave. He didn't believe in any particular religion, or some kind of higher power. Mike believed in odds. Mike believed in playing the numbers. Mike believed in creating his own luck. Mike looked up from the prayer and stared at the sky like a Turkey looking up during the rain. Water droplets were running down his face as he gawked up at the storm. His fatigues had already dampened and absorbed the initial onslaught of the tsunami. The skyline was as black as a cup of freshly brewed Arabica bean coffee.

"Let's move out, men!", Allen said with a commanding authority.

The men huffed it to the Black Hawks and quickly mounted up.

"Let's *Double Time it* to Plum Island!", Allen shouted at the Black Hawk pilot.

The Black Hawk was a tad retro, but it would do the job. There was a thunderous sputtering from the late 80's rotor blades. As the Black Hawk took-off from the landing pad, it shook and jolted the squad. As the team made their approach the flight was starting to get noticeably bumpier. Mike Allen grabbed one of the many hanging support straps and leaned into the cockpit. Luckily, the landing pad was a hop, skip and a jump from Plum Island.

"I hope the return flight has a dinner and a movie," Sergeant Allen shouted to the Pilot crew.

One of the Coasties shot Mike a quick thumbs up and shook his head in disbelief. Allen took that head shake as a sign of disrespect and patted the Coastie on the shoulder.

"How much longer?", he yelled at the pilot. Only to have his question muffled by the cancerous weather. The pilot yelled back at the Sergeant, "We'll have eyes on target in 5 mikes, Sergeant."

71

Sergeant Allen stroked his face with his left hand and held on for dear life with his righthand. This was a low-risk mission, but had huge ramifications on Mike's career outlook. Mike chalked it up to restarting an internet router. As far as he could tell, this was going to be as simple as unplugging a cord from an outlet, waiting 30-seconds and plugging it back in. Flubbing this mission meant getting stepped over once again for a promotion. That was a risk Mike couldn't take. Mike was determined to get the job done, no matter what the cost. The pilot motioned over to Mike Allen and pointed down at the Island.

"Turn up the music!"

The Gunnery Sergeant smiled and clicked the play button on his Mp3 stereo. The Gunnery Sergeant favored old school rock n' roll.

"You ready for this kid?"

"Sir, yes, sir!", Janiwosky shouted back at the Sergeant.

"What about you Corporal? You ready for this?"

"I'm ready for some satisfaction, baby!"

"I'm ready for a whole lotta action, baby!"

"Oh-wee, look out baby for here we come!"

The men performed their pre-mission banter, it was more like a theater troop practicing before a big show. Mike honed in on the humming of the Black Hawk, like a rapper syncing to a metronome before a rap battle. Mike looked to the back of the cargo and noticed that Whitaker was reading a novel.

"What're you reading?", he asked.

Whitaker looked up from his book to answer the Sergeant, "It's one of those *100* books everyone should read before they die."

"Sergeant. We have eyes on target. 1,000 meters out."

"Roger that."

The Black Hawks dropped down to below 500 feet and both teams circled their respective drop points. Each team began to scan the Island for potential threats, signs of distress or anything out of the ordinary. Team Alpha set off for the drop-zone near Fort Terry and Team Bravo set out to main facility. Hernandez looked over to the pilot and pointed out the downed Coast Guard helicopter.

"Down there! That must be the "rescue" chopper!", Hernandez shouted to the team while making quotation marks with his hands to emphasize the sarcasm.

"How fucking auspicious for us," Sergeant Allen said.

"Suspicious? What's suspicious? Other than the fact there is an abandoned Black Hawk occupying our landing zone," Hernandez replied.

"No. Not suspicious. Auspicious you uneducated fuck. How auspicious for us. From the looks of it the Coastie's rescue chopper looks completely unscathed," Sergeant. Allen explained.

"Sorry, Sergeant. I guess I forgot to pack my standard Military Issue word-a-day calendar," Hernandez said jokingly.

Sergeant Allen remained stoic in his disposition. The men could see right through him, he was as transparent as a jelly-fish.

"Let's land this thing. The faster we get in there the

faster we get to go home. If we get back before midnight there's a good chance I get some ass.", Hernandez said.

"That reminds me. How is your sister Hernandez?", Sergeant D'Stefano asked.

The entire crew started bellowing out in laughter. Hernandez just responded by flipping everyone the middle finger. The kind of middle finger that was well pronounced and screamed "Fuck-You".

Hernandez looked over at Kyle Janiwosky. Kyle had his head buried in his knees and looked pretty blue in the face.

"Hey! Hey, new guy!", Hernandez yelled and pointed at the young Corporal.

Corporal Janiwosky barely managed to look up without puking. His face was pale and clammy. The team spilled blood all across the world together, all except Kyle Janiwosky. Kyle was a Pollywog, but the men thought he was alright. D'Stefano made sure to take him under his wing, because the Corporal was the youngest member of the squad and this would be his first re-enlistment working in *Special Operations*.

"Forget about it, kid. This weather is nothing compared to that shit we had to deal with in the *South China Sea*," Hernandez said.

A large gust of wind nearly tipped the chopper to a 35-degree angle. The irony was not lost on Hernandez, he started laughing and barely held on. All the men braced for the relentless onslaught of turbulence.

"Just remember one thing new guy," Hernandez said to the young corporal.

"Yeah? What's that?"

"Slow is smooth and smooth is fast. One wrong move and it's your ass! Just watch your muzzle discipline and you'll be fine," Hernandez explained.

Kyle shook his head and shot Hernandez a receptive thumbs up. Kyle was starting to feel more at home with the squad. The humor acted as a conduit for rapport building within the squad. Hernandez and Janiwosky were singing along to the retro soundtrack like a couple of drunk frat bros at karaoke night. A once contentious relationship had become a bromance of sorts.

"Quit your yapping! We're almost at the LZ," Sergeant Allen proclaimed persuasively.

The Black Hawk maneuvered above the landing zone and hovered right off the coast of the island. The team was spitting distance from Fort Terry. Sergeant Allen slid the cargo door open to get a first-hand look of the ground. From the sky, it looked like the coast was clear.

"Fort Terry. It looks completely dark, sir," Commander Riley said while pointing down from the pilot seat of the *Black Hawk*.

"It's pitch black. I can't see a fucking thing down there," the Co-pilot replied.

"Commander. We need to establish a line of communication before we touch down. Radio the control tower," Mike Allen explained feverishly.

"This is Red Sparrow. Come in, Fort Terry. This is Red Sparrow with Coast Guard Command. Come in, Fort Terry. Fort Terry, do you read me? Over," the Commander desperately attempted to hail the desolate Fort.

The commander radioed the control tower for another five minutes to no avail. The storm was worsening with every passing moment. He noticeably worked to stabilize the Black Hawk. The Black Hawk was listing back and forth, pounded by the brunt of the storm. The storm relentlessly bombarded the helicopter with hurling gusts of wind.

"Sergeant Allen. Fort Terry is completely dark. We have minimal line of sight. We have no response from the Island. Is this mission still a-go?", the Commander asked with a genuinely confused tone.

Mike looked over at Lieutenant Colonel Johnson. Johnson looked back at Mike with this calm intensity about him. The Lieutenant Colonel was seemingly eager to reunite with his former workplace. Mike wanted to make a good impression with the 'company man', so he gave him plenty of authority. He figured the easiest way to make someone feel important was to make them feel important.

Johnson replied, "Mission is a-go. Initial readings show no contamination. No Bio threat detected. Operation Tag Team is mission go."

"You heard him, men. Get ready, boys!. Let's land this bird. Lock and load," Mike ordered the crew.

The Commander swooped into the landing zone, he couldn't wait to put the bird down and flee the storm. The Commander touched down and the team rolled off the black hawk to establish a perimeter.

"Go. Go. Go!"

D'Stefano was the first to depart the helicopter. Followed eagerly by Janiwosky at his rear. Janiwosky lost his footing and planted a knee into the ground. His kneepad plunged almost four inches into the soil. The soil appeared solid from the sky, but to everyone's surprise was an amalgamation of sand, dirt and water. In the process of getting unplugged from the earth Janiwosky unceremoniously decorated the better part of his leg in mud. To save face with the squad, Janiwosky held his rifle at a slanted angle and scanned the beach for hostiles. The team knelt in a concentric circle surrounding the Black Hawk, all spread out about six feet apart. The water was blasting them in the face as each team member began to scan the environment, each of them battle tested and weapons ready. Mike pointed up to the sky and looked at Commander Riley. First Sergeant Allen signaled at the Commander to take off by pointing up and whirling his hand in the air. The Commander saluted back at the Sergeant like two knights about to joust. The Commander pulled back on the yolk and took off into the night sky. As far as he was concerned, he couldn't get off the island fast enough.

"This is Commander Riley to Commander Hodges. Alpha Team has successfully landed on the island. I'm out of here. Over."

"Copy that, Commander. Catch you on the other side," Commander Hodges repeated over the comms.

"Comms check, gentlemen. Sound off," Sergeant Allen ordered.

"Hernandez checking in."

"Reading you loud and clear."

"Janiwosky checking in."

"Reading you loud and clear."

"D'Stefano checking in."

"Loud and clear."

"Whitaker checking in."

"Loud and clear."

"Preach, checking-in."

"Affirmative, comms up."

"Hernandez, front and center. Radio Team Bravo and get me a Sit Rep," Sergeant Allen ordered the Communications Sergeant.

Hernandez knelt down directly adjacent to Mike Allen and began to radio-in Bravo team. He got up and down like an old man, Hernandez had piled on some extra weight over the summer. Normally, his fighting weight was around 185, but these days it was probably closer to 245. He made a large heaving sound as he got down on.

"Bravo Team. Bravo Team. Come in. This is Alpha Team. Over," Hernandez called.

The storm had resumed pummeling the island and began to reclaim the surrounding area. The team braced for impact as the winds came barreling in. A few seconds later their call was answered.

"Copy that. This is Bravo Team. Reading you loud and clear Alpha Team. Over."

"Roger, roger. Begin your reconnoitrer. We're beginning our sweep of the Island. Over and out."

"Roger that. We're making our dissent. We'll have overwatch in 30 seconds. Over."

"Sarge! Bravo Team is aware of our sit-rep and has begun to occupy Landing Zone 2."

"Roger that Sailor," Mike acknowledged.

The island was as quiet as a graveyard at midnight. The mud was as thick as it was heavy like pouring a jar of fresh honey over a bowl of hot fudge. The waves forcefully shattered the rocks around the island. The splashes sounded like a battering ram hitting a door.

"Kyle, go scout out that downed Black Hawk."

Kyle eagerly ran over to abandoned the Coast Guard Black Hawk. The new teammates always ran with a certain extra zeal. That zeal tended to fade over time, but the men appreciated his spirit. Mike learned a long time ago that in this business, the business of War, it pays to be patient.

"It's empty. What am I looking for exactly?", Janiwosky asked.

"Did they leave the keys?", Hernandez said jokingly.

"Sir. No, sir," Corporal Janiwosky replied.

"Well, that's real fucking courteous of the Coast Guard. We got a 20-ton paperweight hogging up space on our landing zone," Hernandez remarked.

"Let's huff it to Fort Terry. Let's *Double Time* it, men. Move out," Sergeant Allen commanded colloquially to the squad.

Tony eagerly obliged and without a moment's hesitation took point for the team. The Fort was less than 1-click from the landing zone. The initial brief on the weather conditions was dead-on-balls accurate. The unlit Fort was barely visible given the weather conditions. The storm was relentlessly adulating around the island. Thunder clamored as Tony led the team to Fort Terry.

Each flash of lightening was followed by a roaring thunder clap. The squadron moved out scanning the environment from head to toe.

As the squad continued to advance on Fort Terry, the weather steadily began to dissipate. There was a momentary respite in the storm. The ingress was short and the men secured several vantage points around Fort Terry. As the men approached the Fort, the rain subsided just long enough to get eyes on target. Each of the men took a knee and aimed their barrels down at Fort Terry. Each keenly scoping out sections of the Fort for signs of life.

"Sir, from the looks of it, I think we're better off just going straight to building 257. I think we should link up with Bravo team and head for the main objective," Hernandez suggested.

Hernandez got up from his prone position and casually unslung his rifle. Clearly, he wasn't taking this situation very seriously. As far as he could tell, this was a no-threat environment and a big waste of time.

"No one is paying you to think Hernandez. Shoulder

your fucking firearm and get back into formation," Sergeant Allen shouted over the comm line.

Sergeant D'Stefano got up from his prone position and strolled over to where Sergeant Allen was standing. Allen grabbed his night vision enhanced binoculars and started investigating the Fort in greater scrutiny.

"Sir, believe it or not, I actually agree with Hernandez on this one. The Fort looks completely deserted," Sergeant D'Stefano said in a disappointed tone of voice.

D'Stefano pulled out his six-inch serrated steel combat knife and started shaving the side of his cheek with it. The blade was damp and covered in cold rainwater. It wasn't a proper shave, more of a nervous tick. Every scrape across his *5-clock* shadow produced a subtle screech, like a rake scraping against concrete. First Sergeant Mike Allen looked to the rest of the team and remained silent to ponder his options. On the one hand, he could hump it over to the main objective and on the other he could waste time exploring the obviously abandoned Fort.

"Hernandez! Front and center. Keep the perimeter

locked down until we get back. Corporal Janiwosky, you've got overwatch. Everyone fall back into position and watch out six. Lieutenant Colonel Johnson, on me," Sergeant Allen said.

The Lieutenant Colonel and Sergeant Allen both ran to the entrance of the Fort. At the entrance there was an empty check-in station. The check-in was only about the size of a prison cell. Mike took his tac-light and flashed it into the check-in. From the looks of it, the check-in had been hastily deserted. Mike and the Colonel advanced further towards the entrance of the Fort. The entrance of the Fort was loosely fortified and full of obvious security shortcomings. Aside from the check-in station, there was a mere six-foot chain-link fence surrounding the perimeter of the Fort. The Fort was about as secure as a run-of-the-mill strip mall.

"Let me guess, the boys back at the Department of Defense figured someone would have to be a complete imbecile to invade an island this close to the mainland, so why bother protecting it? So, why bother outfitting it with any type of serious defense?", Mike asked the Colonel in a somewhat pissed off tone of voice.

"Don't blame me. I just used to work here," Lieutenant Colonel Johnson said in an attempt to deflect the criticism away.

The men strolled on through the perimeter defense check-in station. Each man switched on their LED mounted flashlights and slowly began to scan the exterior of the Fort. The Fort, if you want to call it a Fort, was only two stories tall and made from solid brick.

"So… where to?", Mike asked the retired Colonel.

The Colonel looked over at Mike with an expressionless demeanor. Mike was starting to get an uneasy feeling relying on the Colonel for any level of expertise. He couldn't quite put his finger on it. The Colonel lacked any kind of rapport or tactical presence. The Colonel silently went back to scoping out of the building. Mike quickened his pace and the Colonel followed in kind. The Fort was rather rustic to put it politely. The original structure was built in 1897 and it showed. The outside of the building was covered in a red brick veneer. The building wasn't very imposing up and close.

"I see you spared no expense upgrading the Fort. Clearly OSHA hasn't been doing many site visits," Mike said sarcastically to the Colonel.

The Colonel scoffed at the comment and continued to follow the Sergeant silently. Mike Allen and Lieutenant Colonel Johnson swept the base looking for any sign of intelligent life, neither man was quite sure that existed before the sweep and they were both dead sure it didn't exist after the sweep. Mike ran point and slowly began to sweep his *M4* from room to room. Lieutenant Colonel Johnson had his hand to Mike's shoulder as they breached each room. The Fort was pitch black, not a soul insight. Both men activated their Night Vision goggles as they continued the search of the Fort. Room after room came up empty. There was an ire silence that captured both men's imagination.

"It's… empty," Sergeant Allen said as he slung his M4 over his shoulder. Mike placed his right hand on his hip and lifted his Night Vision goggles with his left. He flipped on his LED flashlight to finish scoping out the control room. At that moment he scoffed and realized Hernandez was right, this Fort was completely FUBAR and it was time to move on to the main objective.

"There's no immediate sign of distress. The armory seems to be full. It's just like everyone abandoned their post," the Lieutenant Colonel noted.

"Let's go report back to the team and get the hell out of dodge," First Sergeant Allen said gleefully.

"Roger that."

The two men fled the Fort like bandits making a hasty escape from a bank heist. As far as Sergeant Allen was concerned, they couldn't get out of there fast enough. Part Sergeant Allen's Special Recon process was always to complete a thorough due diligence of the ground assessment before any direct action. He tapped on the microphone around his throat and radioed the team.

"Men, on me. Converge on the Fort. Double time it to the guard shack at the entrance of the Fort," Sergeant Allen spouted.

The team grouped up around the guard shack just outside of the Fort's entrance. Hernandez was leading the rear and noticeably out of breath. He took a second and hunched over to catch a breather.

"Turns out nobody's home. The Fort is dark. Every station is abandoned. Every desk is empty."

"There are no obvious signs of distress," the Lieutenant Colonel explained.

The men started looking around at each other like a bunch of clergymen when Newton tried explaining gravity for the first time. There was a slight level of disbelief in the Colonel's lack of self-awareness. The men instinctively doubted his credentials based on his target analysis.

"You mean, other than a powerless-abandoned military installation on an island caught in the middle of a tsunami?", Hernandez replied.

"Fuck, Hernandez. Do you ever shut it off?"

Preach took a moment to reflect on the situation, *"He hath filled the hungry with good things; and the rich he hath sent empty away."*

Just as Hernandez was about to spit out a retort, Bravo Team interrupted with a status update breaking the tension.

"Alpha Team. Alpha Team. Do you copy? This is Team Bravo. Over."

"Go for Alpha Team. Over."

"Alpha Team what is your sit-rep. Copy."

"Copy that. Fort Terry is completely abandoned. Over."

"Affirmative. Fort Terry is a fucking ghost town. We have overwatch on top of Building 257, we have your approach covered. From above, the facility looks completely abandoned as well. Over."

"Copy that. We are making our way to you now. Over and out."

The Sergeant removed his gas mask and greased back his hair. Having that plastic suit on made him sweat in all the wrong places.

"We need to radio this in," the Sergeant said and pointed at Hernandez with his index finger fully extended.

"Calling HQ. Calling HQ. This is Alpha team. Do you read me? Over."

"Alpha Team. This is HQ. We're reading you loud and

clear. What's your sit-rep? Over."

"Fort Terry is completely bust. Over."

"Copy that. Any contaminants detected?"

"Negative. Over."

"Any hostile resistance? Over."

"Negative. Over."

"Copy that. Move to primary objective and report back. Over."

"Roger that. Over and out."

"Let's not just stand around with our dicks in our hands. We got a job to do people."

Not a second after Mike shouted his order, the weather worsened sharply as if God herself was warning the squad. It was relentless, unforgiving, an undying storm. The squad charged towards the rendezvous point. Conditions for the approach were suboptimal, but that was the job. The team was racing towards Building 257 at a snail's pace.

"Hailing Alpha Team. Do you Copy? Hailing Alpha Team. Do you Copy? Over."

"Copy that. You are a go for Alpha Team. Over."

"Are you guys hourly or what? What the fuck is taking so long? Requesting a Sit-rep. Over."

"We can't see shit in these Haz Mat suits. We're running knee deep through mud and the rain is obscuring our visibility. Over."

"Roger that. Do you need some Cheese with that wine? Over."

"Copy that Bravo Team. If you'd like to switch places, be my fucking guest. We are up to our asses in mud. Over and out."

"10-4 Alpha Team. We got you covered. Over and out."

Meanwhile on the roof, tempers were high with Bravo Team. The anxiety had started to fatigue the men like a group of drunk friends trying out an Escape Room for the first time. Staff Sergeant Miller was the only one with basic bio-chem mission experience, let alone for a BSL-4 Weapons lab. Aside from that, most of the men just learned about the Island several hours ago. The men were pacing back and forth out of formation, seemingly just stuck on the rooftop in purgatory.

"Overwatch secure, Staff Sergeant," Barnes whispered over the Comm line while scoping out the perimeter of the building.

"Roger that, Marine. Stay frosty."

"All quiet on the western front Staff Sergeant."

"Roger that, Maine."

"Hey Sarge, I thought Sergeant Allen was some kind of badass. What in the hell is taking Alpha Team so damn long?", Lance Corporal Yamada asked.

Staff Sergeant Miller scoffed at the Corporal's flippant remark towards the First Sergeant. The Staff Sergeant had little tolerance for any form sarcasm. He felt it was a form of subordination and not the conduct of a true warrior. The Sergeant was very hands on and got his grimy finger prints on every part of the mission. He was kind of a control freak, probably due to his youth and exuberant inexperience.

94

"By the time you started learning geography in high school, Allen was running Black Ops into countries you've never even read about. He holds the record for the longest unconfirmed kill in military history, a hair inch past Twelve-hundred feet," Miller explained to the talented marksman.

Corporal Barnes immediately regretted his decision and did the smart thing. Which is to say he shut the hell up. Miller crouched down and turned his peering gaze down range through his optical scope.

"Sir, I can't see shit out here," Corporal Barnes noted. The visibility was as obscure as looking out of an old dirty window screen in the middle of a snow storm.

"Stay frosty boys. Just because we can't see nobody doesn't mean nobody can't see us," Miller ordered the team.

Back on the ground, Alpha Team was bogged down in the mud. The Team was approximately *Two-Clicks* outside of building 257. D'Stefano stopped dead in his tracks and took a knee. He motioned to the squad by raising his fist in the air.

"Sir. We have eyes on target," D'Stefano said with contentment.

First Sergeant Allen looked over to Hernandez and signaled him by tapping on the side of his helmet. Hernandez pulled out his tac-radio and began to deliver a Sit-Rep to Bravo Team.

"Hernandez call in our position. I don't want to get fucking shot sneaking up on these guys. Yamada can shoot the wings off a fly from over 1000 yards out," Allen said out of respect for his fellow crewmen.

"Bravo Team. Come in. This is Alpha Team. Over."

"Roger that, Alpha Team. Go for Bravo Team. Over," Staff Sergeant Miller responded swiftly.

"We can see the main facility on the horizon. Confirm receipt of infrared laser. Over."

Allen signaled over to Sergeant Whitaker and then pointed back at Building 257. Whitaker pulled out his infrared laser pointer and ranged it to the target. Whitaker struggled to steady the laser pointer in the high winds. The downpour of water was obscuring his vision and making the laser slip in his hand. He finally managed to steady the laser long enough to get a range.

"Roger that Alpha Team. We've picked up your range finder. You're 1500 yards out. Over."

"Over and out," Hernandez said.

"Alright, let's move out," Allen said.

D'Stefano hopped up from his prone position and advanced towards the main facility. As far as Sergeant Allen was concerned, D'Stefano was probably the most competent marksman of the bunch and had the balls to back it up. There was rarely a mission where he didn't take point for the team. As the men began to work their way towards the objective, D'Stefano decided to drum up some small talk with the crew.

"Did you know that more than 1.5 million Italian Americans enlisted to serve in World War 2? The most of any minority group in America," D'Stefano said while waving his hands in the air.

"Yeah? Did you have any family members that served?", Corporal Janiwosky asked in a curious tone of voice.

D'Stefano was his unofficial mentor and felt that he should get better acquainted. He figured some innocuous small talk was the right way to get that done.

"You know it. My great grandfather Guido D'Stefano enlisted in the Army on June 1st 1940," D'Stefano explained proudly.

The team was trudging along trying to traverse the elements of the island. The monsoon had turned the island into a nominal swamp of muddy sand and decrepit shrubbery. The elements had slowed the team's approach to a literal crawl.

"Which side did your grandfather fight for?", Hernandez asked jokingly.

The team started carnivorously chuckling at D'Stefano's expense. D'Stefano shook his head and responded by saying, "How about you go fuck yourself Hernandez?"

"C'mon. You know I'm just clowning on you, bro," Hernandez replied.

"Hernandez, if I wanted to laugh, I'd follow you into the bathroom and watch you take a piss," D'Stefano said.

"That's a good one. I'll make sure to write that down," Hernandez replied.

D'Stefano shot back a middle finger as stiff as morning wood. As the team approached the objective, they couldn't help but wonder where everyone went. The Island looked completely evacuated, but no one was sure what to make of it all. D'Stefano came to a sudden stop and shouted, "Eyes on the prize gentlemen. We're spitting distance from the objective." The team stood about 50 yards from the target location. Just off to the right side of the entrance.

"Sarge, what do you figure happened here?"

"Nobody's paying you to think Hernandez."

"You know what I think,"

"No. But, I'm sure we're all about to find out,"

"I think we were sent on a giant goose hunt, sir."

"That's an interesting theory."

"Isn't it, though?"

"You know what I think?"

"Sir?"

"I think you should get on that radio and call in our position to Bravo Team."

"Sir, yes sir."

"Corporal Janiwosky, front and center," the First Sergeant ordered the young Marine.

Hernandez squatted down to radio in the team's position. Janiwosky ran over to the Sergeant and stood at attention. His posture was impeccable. He stood upright and ready for his orders.

"Grab a flare out of my backpack," Sergeant Allen commanded the young Corporal.

The Corporal stuck his hand in Sergeant Allen's backpack and started rummaging around for the flare. Allen's backpack was cluttered like a woman's purse after Labor Day.

"Corporal, this isn't a prostate exam. Grab the fucking flare," the Sergeant yelled at Janiwosky. The Sergeant's temper started to boil over and it showed in his demeanor. His normal predictable patience had dissipated to a dull disposition.

"Ah!", the corporal said as he found the flare and pulled it out of the backpack. He held the flare in the air like an Olympic torch runner.

"Sergeant Allen!", Hernandez yelled.

"What is it Hernandez?", the Sergeant replied.

"I can't reach Bravo Team. Comms seem to be down," Hernandez explained.

"What? Impossible. Try again.", Lieutenant Colonel Johnson said in a wary tone.

"I did. Three separate times. All comms are down. There's some kind of static interference," Hernandez explained.

"This is FUBAR. I'm convinced that this place is fucking haunted," D'Stefano said while clutching onto his Italian Horn and Crucifix like an old Italian woman praying at a Church pew.

"Check that shit, you superstitious *A-hole*. Comms go down. Comms go up. It happens," Sergeant Allen explained.

Sergeant Allen grabbed the flare from Janiwosky and started looking it over.

"Janiwosky, have you ever used one of those before?", Sergeant Allen asked while holding the flare in front of Janiwosky's face.

"Sir, No sir," Janiwosky replied.

"It's simple. Snap the top off and wave it in the air. Be careful though, that is a pyrotechnic flare. It emits a bright white light," Sergeant Allen explained.

"Pyrotechnic. Is it dangerous?", he asked.

"Not unless you plan on sticking it up your ass. Get to work solider and pop that fucking flare," Allen said.

Janiwosky popped the flare and started swirling it in a circle. The translucent glow of the flare radiated with a rakish bright white light. The chemical suits reflected the light onto the ground and emanated the ethereal sands of Plum Island.

"Janiwosky, like a rock concert," Sergeant Allen said

admonishingly.

"What?", he replied.

"Side to side, dumbass," Hernandez said while waving his left-hand side to side in a slow swaying motion. Hernandez found the best lessons resulted from a heaping helping of humiliation.

"Ah. Got it," Janiwosky said as he started swaying the flare side to side. He did that for another three minutes until the flare ran down to a stub. The team floundered out of formation waiting for Bravo Team to re-establish comms.

"Hernandez. What's our status on Comms?", the Sergeant shouted in the rain.

Hernandez waived off the Sergeant with his left hand and activated his microphone with his right.

"Bravo Team, this is Alpha Team. Do you copy? Over," Hernandez said.

"Reading you loud and clear, Alpha Team. Over," Sergeant Milled responded in a restless tone.

"Sergeant! We've got Comms back up," Hernandez yelled to Sergeant Allen.

"About fucking time."

"Bravo Team, we have reached the primary objective. Awaiting orders. Over," Hernandez said.

"About fucking time Alpha Team. We breached the facility ten minutes ago. Over," Miller responded nonchalantly.

Sergeant Allen looked over to Lieutenant Colonel Johnson. Johnson trudged over to Hernandez and grabbed the microphone out of his hand.

"What the fuck do you mean 'breached' the facility? Your orders were to cover our approach. Over," Lieutenant Colonel Johnson shouted into the comm line.

"Exigent circumstances, Lieutenant Colonel. Over," Miller replied without remorse.

"Exigent circumstances? What kind of exigent circumstances?", he asked. The retired Lieutenant Colonel clutched onto his revolver and restrained his anger from flaring. The men couldn't understand why he was so perturbed by the news.

"We heard screaming inside the building followed by what sounded like a gunshot. Over," the Sergeant replied.

"Sergeant. You're to hold your position. I say again, you are to hold your position. Do you Copy?"

The line went dead. It was as silent as a cemetery. Apparently, the signal had died once again. The sense of irony was not lost on the squad. It was as layered as a thick Red Velvet Cheesecake.

"Pretty fucking auspicious, right sarge?", Hernandez asked in a snarky tone.

The First Sergeant and the Lieutenant Colonel Broke off from the formation and began to argue amongst themselves for several minutes. They stood just far enough away from the squad to not be heard by the rest of the squad. D'Stefano lifted his right hand up and swirled his finger in a clockwise motion. Janiwosky, D'Stefano, Hernandez, Lindell, and Whitaker circled up into a small group.

"Well…"

"Well, what?"

"Well what? What the hell are we waiting for? Let's rock and roll!"

"Hold your horses, kid. We don't know what we don't know."

"Uh, we have hostiles firing guns. We need to roll up on this place guns blazing and smoke these fools."

"Slow down there kid. We don't have any confirmation of hostiles, yet."

"Hearing a gunshot doesn't mean dick. Until we have confirmed eyes on target, this is still a rescue mission. Do you read me?"

"What'd you figure that's all about?", Whitaker asked as he pointed over to the bickering going on between the Sergeant and the Lieutenant Colonel. It looked like a couple going through a divorce arguing over who gets to keep the dog.

"I… I don't know. I get the feeling our 'intelligence'

sergeant is keeping some mission critical intel from us boys. Take it slow and watch your six. Something doesn't feel right on this job," D'Stefano noted to the team.

"I think we really bought the farm on this one," Hernandez said.

"Looks that way. Stay frosty," D'Stefano responded.

The squad all nodded in agreement and fell back into formation. Whitaker made sure to keep a close eye on the intelligence sergeant. He swiveled his head like an owl scoping out his next meal.

"D'Stefano, lead the way," the Sergeant said as he pointed to the entrance of the facility.

The facility was under constant bombardment from the rain. The visibility was noticeably worsening by the minute. D'Stefano grinned and pulled back the charging handle on his *M4* Carbine. He pointed his rifle forward, left hand on the front grip and right hand on the rear grip. He rested the stock on his right cheekbone and trained his eyes down range.

As the men swept the remainder of the perimeter of the facility, the extreme weather obstructed everything but the facility. As the squad carefully approached the entrance, D'Stefano stopped abruptly and took a knee. He was leading the team by about 10 to 15 yards. The rest of the team slowly caught up and stopped dead in their tracks. The team was at the doorstep of the facility. Building 257 had a massive entrance, the only problem was, the front door was wide open. The men stopped and stared at the entrance in complete silence.

"Colonel… is its standard operating protocol for the front door to be wide-fucking-open during a power outage?"

"Stand fast," the Lieutenant Colonel ordered the squadron.

The Lieutenant Colonel took a deep breath and indignantly holstered his sidearm. The sound of his sidearm rubbing against his damp pleather holster made a loud squish. The signs of exasperation followed the Colonel, like Punxsutawney Phil seeing his own shadow. The Colonel outstretched his arms and put his hands behind his head, like a prisoner about to be handcuffed for a crime he didn't commit. He walked over to Mike Allen. The men noticed his lackadaisical attitude and had no taste for it. The men slowly looked over the entrance of building 257 with a sense of deliberate vigilance and exacting curiosity. The men stood poised and ready with guns drawn at the entrance of building 257. The entrance was two double wide sliding glass doors. One of the doors was marked Exit and the other Entrance.

Overlapping circles from their tactical LED lights loosely covered the entrance of the building and dimly lit the lobby. The rain drops pummeled the men and caused their lights to flicker on and off. Sergeant Allen didn't mind a little bit of luck every now and again, but this gave him cause for pause.

"Should've called the fucking electric company, not a bunch of operators," Hernandez said while preparing to take a better look at the lobby with his night vision goggles.

The facility was dark and the night vision goggles were able to give him some visibility into the lobby. The men stood at the base of the entrance. Even in the middle of a typhoon, there was obvious signs of wear and tear on the building. The building was made of solid concrete and had been severely weathered by the local island conditions and presumably lack of basic maintenance. The building itself wasn't very foreboding. From floor to ceiling, it looked no bigger than a big-box-store. From the outside looking in, the men could only make out a rough outline of the lobby. Something in the lobby piqued his curiosity. Was it a something or a someone?

"Sir..."

"What?"

"There's... there's someone in the lobby."

The men all looked at Hernandez in disbelief. They couldn't tell if he was fucking with them or telling the truth. The rest of the men activated their night vision goggles in order to verify his claim. It took a second to stabilize the goggles, but one by one each man confirmed eyes on target. They couldn't quite make out much more than a shadowy figure lingering in the back of the lobby.

"Eyes on target. In the lobby. A man, unarmed by the looks of it. 50 yards."

"What do we do?"

The men looked at each other, just long enough to break sight with the target. By the time they looked back, the target had vanished from sight.

"Well, that was easy. Maybe next mission, I won't even bring my gun."

"Sir?"

Mike Allen wasn't in the business of making risky decisions. As far as he could tell, this was still a glorified training-op.

"Sir? Am I breaching? What are my orders?", D'Stefano said over the comms.

Mike Allen responded decisively, "Breach."

The men crossed the threshold from the muddy terrain to the hard concrete steps of *Building 257*. The building had six-oversized concrete steps. The Team infiltrated the facility's entrance, led by D'Stefano in a standard 2 by 2 cover formation. Hernandez intuitively looked around the room for a light switch. Each team member scanned the room for survivors. Each team member scanned the room for some sign of life. Each team member scanned the room for something that wasn't there. The room had several large desks and 4 separate doors each marked with a red neon exit sign.

"So… this is it? This is the big-bad BSL-4 Bio Weapons lab?", Hernandez asked the crew.

Each man started investigating the inner workings of the lobby. There was an old commercial grade carpet that made a soggy smushing sound every time someone walked on it. The combination of mud-covered military boots and old carpet made a distinctive sound, like trying to squirt out the last squeeze of a mustard dispenser.

Corporal Lindell could feel his blood pressure start to wane, so he grabbed a candy bar out of front pocket and started peeling back the wrapper. "Ah, Chocolate. Good for every occasion," the Corporal thought to himself. As Lindell fidgeted with the candy-wrapper, it made a loud crinkling that carried throughout the lobby. The rain temporarily subsided and the men turned around in disbelief. They had become familiar with the constant battering of rain drops and hurricane force winds. The men took it as a sign of good fortune, from here on out things were looking up.

"What's the read out looking like?"

Whitaker glanced over at his handy dandy *High Volume Aerodynamic Particle Sizer.* This was his first encounter with the device. On the ride over he had a chance to peruse through the lengthy owner's manual. He gave it a second to update the reading and impatiently tapped it on the side, like an old videogame cassette that wouldn't load.

"Particle size distribution looks completely normal. Nothing out of the ordinary as far as I can tell. That is aside from the disserted bio weapons lab," Whitaker called out to the Sergeant.

Mike Allen let out an enormous sigh of relief and went back to investigating the lobby of the laboratory.

"From this point on, respirators and Hazmat suits on. I'm still not 100% convinced anything actually happened here. First objective is to find Dr. Kerrigan. If we beat Bravo team to the objective, drinks are on me tonight," Sergeant Allen spouted to the men.

One by one the men dropped their gear bags and began to suit up. The Haz Mat suits made a crunching sound like the crinkling of a potato chip bag.

Meanwhile on the upper deck, Sergeant Miller led Bravo team into the corridors of the top floor of *Building 257*. The sound of a gunshot snapped his instincts into full gear, kill switch engaged. The young Staff Sergeant had a chip on his shoulder and was eager to climb the chain of command. The easiest way to do that was putting the pedal to the metal and find Dr. Kerrigan before Alpha Team.

"Sir, I recommend we suit up," Barnes said affirmatively while pulling out his gear bag.

The Staff Sergeant stopped dead in his tracks. The rest of the team abruptly halted their vigorous progress towards the sound.

"What's the read out?", the Staff Sergeant inquired. His tone of voice was deliberate, as if he wanted to undermine the Medical Sergeant's advice. Corporal Barnes was unphased and would not let a cavalier superior officer deter his sound Medical advice.

"Readout is normal. *No* Bio hazards detected," Corporal Barnes read aloud from the *High-Volume Aerodynamic Particle*.

Unfortunately for the team this only re-affirmed the Staff Sergeant's suspicions about the veracity of the mission. As far as he could tell, this was a disgruntled employee with a gun or a blown circuit breaker.

"Men, as far as I can tell. This is probably just another case of workplace violence. We have overwatch and the element of surprise. Every second we waste up here is one second less we have to take the initiative. We are to proceed on mission and take the objective. Move out."

"Sir...", Barnes whimpered in pathetic protest.

The Staff Sergeant swiveled his head around on its axis, like someone spinning a globe for the first time. The Staff Sergeant glared at the Medical Sergeant with an indigent intimidating intense look on his face. The Staff Sergeant's patience was wearing thin and it showed on his face. His forehead was swelling with a blood red hue like a ripened tomato ready to be plucked from the vine. There was a vein thumping and extruding from his neck.

"Every second we stand here is one less potential hostage and one more potential body bag. We're moving out," the Staff Sergeant said in a disparaging tone.

The Medical Sergeant had a choice to make. On one hand he could continue his protest, or on the other hand he could just get inline and follow his orders. The Medical Sergeant was old school. He often chose the path of most resistance, to his own detriment. He often chose the path of learning the hard way. He often chose the path that prevented him from climbing the ranks. For once, the Medical Sergeant chose to let cooler heads prevail and follow orders.

"I-I-Sir, yes sir."

The Medical Sergeant's momentary hesitation increased the heighted state of awareness adorned by the rest of the squad. The Medical Sergeant slung his rifle and unholstered his sidearm. He held his M9 Baretta out with his righthand and the *High-Volume Aerodynamic Particle* in his left hand. The Medical Sergeant began to purposely slow his pace like a marathon runner trying to catch his second wind. He steadily fell behind the squad. Barnes had garnered no favor with the squad by voicing his concerns. The hallways had no real rhyme or reason to the design. The men traversed a labyrinth of long thin corridors with near twenty-foot ceilings. The tile floor occasionally glistened as the beams of the LED mounted flashlights hit the ground. The men covered the hallway with their M4 Carbines. Each man moved in a straight line and slowly scanned the room. The military was like that, full of rigorous and repeatable processes to follow.

118

Those who followed the processes the best tended to get promoted the fastest.

The men hastened the search and began to increasingly pull away from the Medical Sergeant. At this point, the men had penetrated deep into the facility. At this point, then men had not seen a single soul. At this point, this was starting to feel like a wild goose chase. Room by room the squad cleared the upper deck of the facility. No guns, no germs, no one to be found. The Staff Sergeant stood in the center of one of the cleared-out rooms with his hands tucked under his armpits. The normal protocol for this sort of situation would be to radio in to command with a Sit-Rep.

"No sign of Dr. Kerrigan. She's probably in the basement attempting to get the reactor back on," the Staff Sergeant explained logically.

To the young Sergeant the simplest answers tended to be the most correct answers. The world wasn't some mystifying confound, life was as simple as lead, follow or get out of the way.

"Sir?"

"What is it, Yamada?"

"Shouldn't we radio are Sit-Rep in to HQ?"

"This isn't a fucking Democracy, Yamada."

Clang. Clang. Clang.

The Staff Sergeant yelled to the team, "Listen up."

The squad pivoted towards the noise with guns drawn towards the hallway adjacent to the room. There was a door off-center across from the open door of the room. Something was making noise on the other side. The sign above the door read, "Stairwell". The door signs flickered using what last ounces of emergency power they could latch on to. The men slowly exited the room and surrounded the door of the hallway. This was it, time to turn it up. Sergeant Miller pulled out a wrecking bar and handed it over to Yamada. He plunged the wrecking bar into the door jam. He obstructed the line of fire for the other men, so they held up their rifles. Subsequently, this took all light off the breaching point. The Corporal used all of his strength and pried the door open with his wrecking bar. The men quickly pointed their rifles back at the door to identify and engage any possible threat.

"Woahhh! Don't shoot! Friendly!", a man said while holding his forearms up to shield his eyes from the bright light of the LED flashlights pointed in his face.

"Identify yourself!", Staff Sergeant Miller hollered at the unknown man.

"Don't shoot! I'm one of the fishermen. We washed up on shore during the hurricane. What a GD nightmare," he said.

The Sergeant stepped up to the man and ripped his forearm down from his face. He wanted to get a better look and see who he was dealing with. The Sergeant took a quick minute and sized him up. At first glance, he seemed like one of the fishermen. He had mangy hair, an unkept beard and looked seaworthy.

"What the fuck are you doing pounding on the door like that?"

"The doors have these automatic locking mechanisms from the inside. I ran up the stairs once I heard you guys. And... I just tried to call for help."

"Mhmm. That doesn't explain what you're doing up

here by your lonesome. Start talking," Sergeant Miller ordered the man. Miller was wet behind the ears, but didn't lack a sense of paranoia and cunning.

"What am I---? I—", the man stuttered stupendously.

Miller wanted to cut right to the point. He was a man on a mission and this guy was only wasting his time.

"Where's Dr. Kerrigan?", he asked while shining his light back in the man's face. Instinctively the man raised his hand up to block the light from obstructing his view.

"*Oh*. Doctor Kerrigan. Yeah. She's down in the basement with everyone else, trying to get the power back on or something… It's all a little above my paygrade, you know?", he explained in a soft tone.

The squad nestled their firearms away for the moment, this all seemed to be a run of the mill power outage. Miller's earlier suspicions were confirmed and he was more eager than ever to link up with Dr. Kerrigan.

"Who are you guys? Are you here to help with the power outage? Or…"

"We're the cavalierly, son. Don't get in our way and you

won't have a problem," Miller said while shoving the beleaguered fisherman to the side of the stairwell. Miller shoved the fisherman aside like a varsity football jock shoving his way through an overcrowded locker room of freshmen.

"Sure thing. I'm just glad you're here. Follow me. I'll show you the way to the basement," he said as he stuck his arm out. He looked more like a doorman at a fancy hotel lobby rather than a shipwrecked fisherman.

The Sergeant paused for a moment and stuck his head over the railing to get a better look down the stairwell. He grabbed half a dozen glowsticks out of his pocket and started activating them one at a time. Every time he cracked a glowstick he shook it and tossed it down the stairwell. The green neon light began to illuminate the once pitch-black stairwell.

Meanwhile, inside the main facility from the ground floor level.

"Sir. We've got survivor here by the looks of it," Hernandez said and pointed his flashlight over at a body on the floor. Mike swiveled his rifle and pointed it in the direction of one of the survivors. Mike was perplexed. He couldn't figure out if the survivor was a friend or foe. From the looks of it the survivor was part of the Fishing Crew that washed ashore.

Lindell slowly approached the survivor to assess the damage. He often acted on pure instinct like a mama bear looking out for her cubs. Lindell checked for a pulse, flipped over the limp body and placed his ear on the chest of the survivor. After about 10 seconds of silence a smirk gleamed across Lindell's face. He raised his hand and shot the crew a thumbs up. Lindell rolled up the sleeve of the survivor to find a spot to inject an adrenaline syringe. As he began to roll back the sleeve, he spotted something. Something he hadn't seen in quite some time.

"You've got to be shitting me," he said under his breath.

The Team looked over curious at Lindell's statement. Lindell wasn't much for profanity, nor hyperbole. When he partook in colorful language, the men noticed.

"What is it?", Mike questioned him.

"Look for yourself," he said holding up the left wrist of

the survivor.

Mike examined the pale arm of the survivor only to see a large blackened skull adorned with a *Green Beret and bayonet knife*.

"Interesting…"

"What is it Sarge?"

"Looks like we have a former Special Operator over here. Green Beret from the looks of it. So, the plot thickens," Sergeant Allen said suggestively.

Mike Allen uncomfortably coughed through his respirator. He instinctively raised his hand in order to cover the cough. The Retired Colonel finally decided to chime in, "Sergeant the new *CDC* recommended protocol for covering a cough or sneeze is to use your elbow, not your hand."

"Yeah Sarge, get with the times," Hernandez said jokingly.

The squad looked over at the Retired Colonel with a significant level of incertitude. Hernandez buddied up with D'Stefano and whispered, "Is this guy for real?

What a fucking dweeb."

D'Stefano shrugged off the comment and went back to scanning the hallway. Whitaker slowly walked over to Sergeant Allen's position. His boots made loud thuds as he walked down the hallway, it sounded like someone serving a Tennis Ball at 100 miles per hour.

"Does this mean anything to you?", Whitaker asked the Intelligence Officer suspiciously. He looked the Intelligence Officer dead in the eyes. Whitaker wanted to gauge his honest reaction, even if it was from behind a face shield and a respirator. Whitaker wasn't a beat-around the bush kind of guy. He focused crisply in on the Colonel's state of mind like a dog staring a bowl of food.

"No... I can't say that it does."

"Can't or won't?", Whitaker replied to the wishy-washy answer.

The Intelligence Officer wasn't amused by Whitakers snarky disposition. He wasn't akin to being challenged or second guessed.

"Do I have to pull rank, sailor?"

That chicken-shit kind of response gave Whitaker enough gusto to muscle up on the Colonel. Whitaker smiled and said, "Look I don't care who you were years ago, or who you are now, or whose Nephew you used to be…"

The crew was stunned by his words. Occasionally, everyone popped off, but rarely, if ever did anyone except that to come from the ever cool, calm and collected Whitaker. The tension in the room was as thick as freshly churned Irish Butter.

"Gentlemen, please. Why don't we just ask our sleeping beauty over here?", Lindell said as he plunged the adrenaline needle into the arm of the Mercenary. Lindell emptied the contents of the syringe into the forearm of the Mercenary. It took almost instant affect and the Mercenary slowly regained consciousnesses.

Sergeant Allen knelt down to meet the Mercenary at eye level. The Mercenary had barely begun to wake when a large snarl rang out. It was followed by the calamity of what could only be a fire fight. The Sergeant hopped up

127

from a kneeling position and pulled his sidearm out. He scanned both ends of the hallway, the men sprang into action ready for a skirmish. The men couldn't make heads or tails of the direction of fire. Was it above or below? Was it behind or in front? The hallways were narrow and tall, which made for the perfect processionary confusion.

CLACK. CLACK. CLACK.

"Who fired their weapon? Give me status."

To the chagrin of the Sergeant, no answer came across the comms. The room was as silent as a library on a Sunday afternoon.

CLACK. CLACK. CLACK.

"Who engaged? Does anyone have eyes on target?"

The Sergeants question lingered unanswered as the squad covered both ends of the hallway and attempted to determine the source of the gunshots. The Team was as attentive as a dog trying to follow a laser pointer.

"It's Bravo Team, sir," the Gunnery Sergeant answered.

It was a familiar sound that the entire squad was able to easily recognize. Nothing else had such a robust and distinctive sound to it than the a 5.56×45mm NATO, air-cooled, gas-operated, direct impingement, magazine-fed, select fire M4 carbine.

"Sir…"

"Hernandez! Get on the comms and figure out what the fuck is going on with Bravo Team."

"Sir…"

"What!?"

"Sir, we need to pursue," Whitaker spoke up with an inquisitiveness of a child discovering caffeine for the first time. He knew with each passing moment the odds of successfully interceding diminished exponentially.

"Negative, sailor. Belay that order," the Intelligence Officer said from across the room.

The crew looked over at the Intelligence Officer in a furious disbelief at his cowardice.

"Bravo Team could be on any level of this facility and

we cannot risk a firefight. Our objective is to find Dr. Kerrigan and turn the reactor back on. We need to restore power ASAP. For now, Bravo Team is on their own…"

D'Stefano slung his rifle over his shoulder, pulled his combat knife from his boot and charged the Intelligence Officer. To which the Intelligence Officer pulled his sidearm and racked back the slide. It did not have the intended effect of intimidating the Gunnery Sergeant. The Intelligence Officer prudently holstered his weapon and said something that halted D'Stefano dead in his tracks.

"If we don't get that reactor back online the building will collapse on itself…"

CLACK. CLACK. CLACK.

The men were completely unphased by the sounds of their comrades most likely engaged by hostiles. The words of the Intelligence Officer obscured any attentiveness or vigilance left in the squad. D'Stefano sheathed his knife and folded his arms in protest.

"I thought that was only a failsafe," Allen said.

"How do you think the failsafe is triggered? By this very fucking scenario. Why do you think the front door was open?", the Colonel said in an admonishing tone of voice.

"How much time do we have?", D'Stefano asked the Colonel.

"We have two hours, max. If we're lucky, two and a half."

"Bravo Team, come in. Bravo Team, come in," Hernandez continued his attempt to hail Bravo Team over the comm line.

CLACK. CLACK. CLACK.

Hernandez was helplessly fidgeting with this radio and failed to reach the other squadron of men. The thick steel and concrete of the building obscured the radios. The radios were about as effective as using a Chinese finger trap as a condom.

"Sergeant!", Hernandez shouted.

"What?"

To everyone's delight a scrambled transmission muttered across the radio.

"Al-pha Tea-m, this is Sergea-nt Miller. Come, in…", Sergeant Miller pleaded over a broken communication relay.

"Copy that. We heard gunfire. Over."

"We---", the Sergeant said over a garbled transmission.

"Repeat. Bravo Team. Repeat. Come in. Shit!", Hernandez shouted over the comm line.

"Weeeeeave breached sub-basement level 1… via the main stairwell. Over," he said as the transmission waned in and out of favor.

"Copy that. What are we up against? Over," Hernandez pleaded with the Staff Sergeant.

"We found a lone survivor from the fishing boat. Son of a bitch jabbed me with something. A fucking syringe full of god knows what! Little shit retreated into the biolab," he said while heavily breathing.

"Status Report?"

"We lost Barnes in the commotion, but I think we managed to wound the bastard in the process. Over," he said with bated breath. The Sergeant's voice was becoming somewhat erratic.

Hernandez held the speaker up for the rest of the team to listen. The squad was tuned in to the fleeting conversation. Each man stared with a tunnel vision at the headset as the Staff Sergeant screamed bloody murder over the microphone.

"Yeah… We tagged him alright. There's a trail of blood. We're in pursuit. Over and out," the Sergeant shouted through the comm like a hound picking up the trail of a hair.

Meanwhile in the upstairs level of the building. Corporal Barnes had thought it prudent to fully suit up. He intentionally fell back as the squad proceeded further the bio weapons lab to chase the fisherman. Just as Barnes finished suiting up he heard a rustling sound, like the scurrying of a rat running across the floor. He pulled the muzzle of his rifle to the corner of the room and shined a light in the direction of the noise. To his surprise nothing was there. To his surprise nothing was afoot. To his surprise nothing was out of the ordinary.

"I got to get the fuck out of this place," he said aloud to
an empty room.

"Barnes. Can you read me?", Sergeant Miller shouted
over the Bravo Teams comm line.

Barnes thought it best to sit back and let his squad leader
do all the heavy lifting. No matter how uncharacteristic
of Barnes, he felt that the Sergeant was on a collision
course with getting everyone killed or worse,
accidentally unleashing a bio weapon from the lab.
Barnes turned off his radio and transmitter. From this
point out, he was on his own or would link up with
Alpha Team.

Barnes began to follow the trail of tears left behind by
his comrades in arms. As he progressed deeper into the
facility he marked his position by drawing a big smiley
face on the wall with a luminescent paint he kept handy.
It easily showed up on his night vision goggles. As he
was marking a wall next him another scurrying sound
rushed by the adjacent unmarked hallway. He swiveled
his head and turned his M4 towards the open door.

134

"Whose there?"

Barnes ditched the heroic bullshit and bravado from his earlier protest. He turned his radio back on with his left hand and held his rifle with this right. The light was shaking up and down. He fumbled about trying to multi-task or calm his nerves enough to steady the rifle.

"Sergeant. This is Barnes. Do you copy?"

The Sergeant did not respond to his plea. He was met with unyielding silence.

"Anyone on this channel. Do you copy?"

"Barnes? This is Alpha team. We read you loud and clear. Over," Hernandez responded affirmatively.

"Whew! I thought one of you fuckers was up here messing with me...", Barnes said in relief. He momentarily could relax and shake off his intolerable sense of anxiety. His respirator was fogging up and obscuring his vision. He decided to remove it and take a second to reset. He dropped his gun and the began to remove his respirator.

"I'm on my way to you...", he said followed by

inaudible screeching and static noises.

"Barnes?!?! Do you copy?", Hernandez pleases with his comrade.

"Fuck! Why are these comms so unreliable?", Hernandez shouted.

Sergeant Allen was somewhat flustered with the lack of progress and lack of communication.

"Whitaker, front and center."

"Sir?"

"Grab our guest and follow me," he said.

The time for indecision had passed. The time for playing it by the book had passed. The time for not making choices had passed. The Sergeant racked his rifle and pointed it forward down the hallway. Whitaker grabbed the wounded fisherman by the arm and swung the near lifeless body over his shoulder. Whitaker was large enough to hold his rifle in one hand and manage the survivor with the other. The men swept the first floor of the building and headed towards Corporal Barnes, or at least, where they thought he was.

Chapter 4: Blood Money

Jason clasped the rearview mirror with his cartoonishly large right hand and slanted it downward. After a quick glance he said, "Boss, I think we got company."

Dirk instinctively looked back and flipped his sunglasses on the back of his head. Dirk stared down the abutting vehicles and said, "We have a tail alright."

"How far boys?", Maddox asked.

Jason took some chewing tobacco out with his left hand and gripped the wheel with his right hand.

"Eyes on target. *One Hundred Yards* and closing. About four cars back. What am I doing here, boss?", Jason asked while fondling his 45.

"Change lanes. Make it obvious," Maddox said.

Jason slammed on the brakes and switched over to the left adjoining lane. As we changed lanes the SUV followed in kind, but in a much less abrupt manner.

"We got a cool customer here," Jason said.

Dirk drew his 45 Caliber revolver from his waistband, just one of the many firearms he concealed on his person, and pointed it over the backseat at the approaching SUV. Luckily for us, our SUV was covered in black 'limo-tint' windows.

"What am I doing? Boss?", Dirk asked.

"Keep your pants on Dirk. Just drive. Act normal. It's probably just an advanced security detail for the shot-caller. Don't pop-off just yet," Maddox explained with a calm precision.

The team drove for another ten or fifteen minutes, slowly meandering towards the general direction of the meet site. The SUV was stuck on them like a cheap suit on a Cop. Jason kept his cool, typical Jason. He rolled down the window and spit some of his chew out. Most of the chew flung off onto the rear driver side window. It was a rather disgusting habit, but it calmed his nerves.

"Boss, these guys are still on us. Want me to lose em?", Jason asked politely and casually.

Clearly, he was starting to get impatient with Maddox's conservative indecision. Jason looked in the mirror at

Maddox and then over to Dirk.

"Burn 'em," Maddox said.

"Buckle up," Jason said with a smile.

Dirk clicked the safety back on his revolver and tucked it into his waistband. They each strapped on their belts and held on for dear life. Jason slammed on the brakes and drifted into an alleyway like a Tokyo rice rocket. The other SUV lazily rolled down the road and noticeably gave up its pursuit.

"Hmm. That was easy," Dirk said in a slightly disappointed tone.

"Yeah. It was," Maddox replied while keeping a watchful eye on the side mirror.

"Yeah. A little too easy," Jason said equally as disappointed as Dirk.

Jason pulled the car over a few blocks down the road. We slowly came to a stop and Dirk asked, "Are we there yet?"

Jason just shook his head; it comes with the territory.

Jason and Maddox served multiple deployments in Afghanistan, Iraq and who knows how many private security details. Dirk was plucked straight out of the Ranger Core.

"I'm waiting on a confirmation from the contact," Maddox said.

Jason kept his hands on twelve and two with his head on a swivel. The three mercenaries waited eagerly for a rendezvous point. Dirk started tapping his hands on his knee caps, like a drummer who couldn't find his rhythm.

Ding! Ding!

"Meet at the Montauk Harbor in 45 minutes," the text message read.

"Montauk Harbor, boys. Double time it!", Maddox shouted.

Maddox vigorously started typing back, "How do you expect us to make that trip in 45 minutes?"

"With fancy driving skills like that, I have the utmost faith in your abilities," the text read.

141

We drove like a bat out of hell and before we knew it, there was the Montauk Harbor. It wasn't much to look at, the trio was thoroughly unimpressed with the meeting spot. Though, it wasn't the shadiest place to meet, it had a small town feel to it. Jason slowed his approach and started scoping out exits.

"Boss, this is a hell of a place to do business," Jason said sarcastically. What he probably meant to say is that this place was a great place to get ambushed.

"No kidding. One way in and one way out. I love it. Just like the OK Corral!", Dirk said in a cocky tone of voice.

"Don't worry so much. We're stateside meeting with a Civilian Contractor. What could possibly go wrong?", Maddox asked.

"Yeah, I don't like it. Reminds me of that job we did in Karachi," Jason protested.

It was just past dusk, but the harbor was oddly emptied out for this time in the day. We parked the car in a very open part of the parking lot. We had our veritable pick of the litter when it came to parking spaces. The parking lot was at the end of a long-gated entry way that was adjacent to the docks. Dirk couldn't wait to get out of the car and stretch his legs. He jumped out as soon as the car stopped moving. Jason took a second to adjust the mirrors and scout out some escape routes. They all got of the car and waited in the middle of that parking lot. And waited. And, waited some more.

"What's the deal?", Dirk said.

"Boss, you know this guy or what?", Jason inquired.

"Only by reputation," Maddox replied.

The mercenaries sat there for about three hours; it was like watching a bunch of used car salesman waiting for a customer to show up on the car lot. The contact simply went by the name Billy. A mutual friend recommended them to Maddox and heard Billy was looking for some discrete low budget operators. He also heard Maddox's team was stateside looking for work.

Jason strolled the docks, constantly scoping out for any indication Billy was actually going to show up. Jason found refuge squatting on the top of the storage container to get some kind of overwatch. Dirk was sitting on the dock of the bay skipping rocks into the ocean. Maddox was just content watching the boats float on by and waiting for the inevitable arrival of the contact. Dirk sprouted up, made his way back to the car and slammed his hands on the hood.

"Boss! Let's get out of here. This guy ain't going to show. We got played."

Whistle!

Jason let out a large howling whistle and hopped down from the empty storage container. A plum of dust shot up as he landed, he must've been weighing in close to around 300 pounds these days.

"Boss! Twelve o'clock! Look sharp, we got company."

"Talk to me," Dirk said as he started scanning the main drag.

"Three extra-large Black Luxury type SUVs 400-500 yards out. Coming in hot," Jason explained.

Dirk jumped up on the hood of the car to get a better look. He put one hand over his brow and another around the handle of the nickel-plated 1911 tucked into his waist band.

"Calm the fuck down," Maddox ordered the oafish mercenary.

After their last job, running point on a security detail in Sierra Leone, Maddox could tell, it took a toll on Jaron and Dirk. Operating stateside was just the change in pace the team needed. As far as Maddox new this was some cushy security detail for a spoiled *Billionaire Defense Bro*. The SUV's rolled up and hard braked about ten feet from the team. The SUV's encircled the team like a crescent moon. A small unassuming man hopped out of the back seat of the forward vehicle. He was about Five-Feet-Five-Inches, had a shiny bald cul-de-sac on top of his head and thin framed wire reading glasses.

"Ah! The Three musketeers! On guard!", Billy said as he put his fists up and 'play' punched at the team. He did that awkward back and forth fencing style punch routine, typical corporate stooge kind of bullshit. Jason scoffed and looked away. Dirk snickered and played along for a moment. Maddox stood stoic, but eager to strike up a conversation.

"*Man.* You guys look wound up tighter than a girder belt around a minister's daughter. What's the matter?", Billy inquired.

Jason stepped forward closer to the shot-caller, he took about three long strides and asked, "What's the matter? We've been waiting here for three fucking hours. What's the job?"

Billy smiled and asked, "Didn't you're mother ever teach you that good things come to those who wait?"

Maddox placed a hand on Jason's shoulder, it was a subtle way to let Jason know to calm the fuck down. Maddox had a distinctive grip, like a parent redressing their spoiled child.

"Now… which one of you is the famous "Mad Dog" Maddox? I wonder?", Billy inquired to the group of mercenaries.

Jason and Dirk both simultaneously pointed to Maddox and Maddox stepped to the forefront of the trio. Maddox wasn't shy about being the team lead, nor sheepish when it came to stepping into a hot-zone. The way Maddox figured it, it came with the territory.

"Ah? You're Mad Dog Maddox?", Billy said with a

slightly disappointed tone of voice.

"I go by, Maddox, just Maddox. And, that must make you Billy the kid? I take it," Maddox asked.

Billy simply beamed a smile back at Maddox without answering the Mercenaries inquiry. He stood there with this big goofy look on his face, like a person who didn't know how to take a joke but smiled anyways. There was this long awkward pause only to be characteristically interrupted by Dirk.

"Let's get down to business. Shall we?", Dirk asked. Dirk had his hands around his waist. Jason with his hands firmly tucked took into his arm pits.

Billy continued, "Ah, yes! Your reputation precedes you. You guys really don't mess around? I like that. Just the kind of team we need for this job. A team with true grit and Moxy for days."

Billy smiled and pulled out a stick of bubble gum like a kid in a candy store. He wadded it up and started obnoxiously chewing it. He discarded the wrapper on the ground and started sizing up the team. Dirk slowly moved his head to the right looking for any kind of que from Maddox. Maddox was stone cold. Dirk re-focused his concentration on the other vehicles.

"We're running a series of external safety audits for one of our top facilities. The contract is up for re-negotiation, congressional oversight and what not. Look don't worry about the nitty-gritty," Billy explained hastily.

"What's the job?", Maddox asked.

Billy snapped his fingers and one of his large goons stepped out of the SUV holding a titanium plated briefcase. His bodyguard had two large bulges, one on each side of his chest. Clearly, this guy was packing some serious hardware. The goon handed each of the team members a large manilla file folder, which had a mission dossier.

"The job… the job is Building 257," Billy explained to the curious operators.

A look of confusion and ignorance overwhelmed the team. The curiosity got the better of them and each team member opened up the Mission Dossier for further inspection.

"Ha! Plum Island?", Maddox reacted after reading the first page of the dossier.

"C'mon, man!", Dirk said jokingly.

Jason threw his hands up and walked around in a small circle. He put his hands on his waist and started kicking the gravel on the parking lot. Kind of like a child waiting for his parents to pick him up from school.

"You want us to invade Plum Island?", Jason asked.

"No, no, no. Nothing so serious. Nothing so official. Nothing so dramatic. We you to participate in a minor stress test on the facility infrastructure and defensive capabilities. Our security contract is in jeopardy. Now-a-days everyone wants to cut the defense budget, for this, that or the other reason. It's the trendy thing to do in Congress. It really earns you a lot of brownie points with joe-shcmo concerned citizen. Somehow Congress got this idea that you'd have to be a complete idiot to invade Plum Island. So, why bother spending tax payer dollars protecting it?"

"Wonder how they got that bright idea?", Dirk asked sarcastically.

149

"What's the job, Billy?", Maddox asked.

Dirk shook his head and hurled his cigar into the river. Billy grinned and tipped his $1000 oval shaped aviator sun glasses down onto the brim of his nose.

"Like I said, this is a simple job. We need to test the facility security, blah, blah, blah," Billy explained nonchalantly.

"Why do I get the distinct feeling you're not telling us everything?", Jason asked the contractor.

Billy stroked his dainty beard and said, "This job is right up your alley. It's a simple snatch and extract."

"Nothing's simple when you're talking about infiltrating a Government Bio Weapons Lab," Maddox interjected.

"Let alone… a facility on an island," Maddox said while perusing the dossier.

"Who's the target?", Dirk asked.

"It's not a who, it's a what," Billy replied.

Maddox glanced to his right to gauge Jason's expression. Jason had the dossier folded up under his arm pit. Maddox swiveled over to the left and Dirk had his hands around his waist. Clearly, neither one of them was thrilled with the assignment.

"What's the target?", Jason asked.

Billy scoffed at the question, "How uncharacteristic for a merc? What do you care?"

"I care, because I need to know the transport protocols," Jason explained.

"Nothing too serious," Billy said.

"From my understanding, the only thing they deal with on Plum Island is Category A Bio Weapons," Maddox said.

Jason and Dirk both looked over at Maddox in amazement. Neither man had experience handling biological contagions.

"Yes, that is mostly correct," Billy replied.

"Mostly?", the trio said in unison, like a barbershop quartet singing around a bon fire.

"The facility is carrying a relic, a throwback experiment

from World War 2. Albumin…", Billy explained. Billy trailed off for dramatic effect. It worked, because Dirk jumped in on him.

"Why are you saying that like we know what it is?", Dirk asked.

Jason pulled Maddox in close and whispered, "It's harmless. Albumin is basically just a protein in your blood."

Billy started a slow ironic golf clap and a shit eating grin beamed across his face. Billy was still obnoxiously chewing his buddle gum. From the looks of it the gum was some kind of nicotine laced chewing gum.

"Congratulations Jason, you can read the dossier," Billy said while sarcastically clapping.

"I was a combat medic for six years you asshole. Of course I know what Albumin is," Jason belligerently said to Billy.

Three other bodyguards jumped out of the SUV's, each of which carrying Russian made AK-47s. The team didn't flinch, it was just a precaution, nothing to worry about. Jason wasn't easily intimidated, but checked his tone out of respect.

"Jason do us all a favor and keep reading the dossier," Billy said politely.

"Well, it's not just any albumin, it was an experimental batch of albumin mixed with gonane, Testosterone and Adrenaline. In order to create…", Jason read aloud to the group and stopped abruptly at the drug's stated purpose. Jason looked up at Billy with this bewildered expression on his face. All of the color drained from his face.

"That's right. It's not a typo. Read it," Billy explained.

"To create… a Super Solider Serum," Jason said.

"Bingo! The chemical was delightfully named the SSS-1. Give the Army creativity points on that one. Am I right?"

This all seemed rather fantastical in nature to the team. A defense contractor wanted us to invade an Island in order to justify his bloated Defense Contract and somehow make out with a 60-year-old Super Solider Serum.

"I know what you're thinking. Sneak into a secret

military BSL-4 Bio Weapons Lab, snatch an archaic super solider serum and find a way back to the mainland without a scratch. Sounds impossible, right?", Billy asked.

"I mean, yeah. That is exactly what I was thinking," Maddox responded.

"Look, this is just a stress test on our security. You sneak into the facility with some kind of beach incursion or better yet, a wrecked boat off the coast of Plum Island. Two of you distract the guards, which operates on a skeleton crew over the weekend and one of you find a way into the lab, snatch the SSS-1, by the time the Coast Guard shows up to "rescue" the crew, you'll make out like bandits," Billy casually explained to the operators like someone explaining the parking situation at a rock concert.

"Other than skeleton crew of security guards what are we talking about? What's the head count?", Maddox asked.

"Oh, there's about 400 staff on the island. A normal weekend, probably a quarter of that figure at best. The island is *over* 800-suqare miles. For the most part people should be pretty well spread out. Remember the island is just a façade. The Weapons Laboratory goes well below the surface of the earth," Billy explained.

"You want one of us to sneak past 100 or so people? On an island that is 800 square miles?", Dirk asked with some hesitancy.

"Trust me. It'll be easier than you think. The facility was originally built some *Seventy* or so years ago. Over that time there was a patch work or lazily put together security features. I mean, the infrastructure is old as dirt," Billy explained.

"What kind of resistance can we expect?", Dirk asked.

"On the water, there is a single Coast Guard Patrol of the island by boat," Billy explained.

"One boat patrol? You serious?", Dirk asked.

"Yes. A single Patrol boat after hours," Billy replied somewhat menacingly.

"A single boat patrol guarding a BSL 4 Weapons Lab?", Jason asked.

"Just one. On mainland America, the government is barely functional on the weekend. Mind you that is during normal tide. When you ship out tonight, we're expecting hurricane like winds and waves up to 15 feet. Odds are there might not even be a single patrol out tonight," Billy replied.

The team started slowly shaking their heads in agreement. Maddox was on the fence, Dirk was gun-ho about the mission and Jason wasn't convinced. Jason was inherently skeptical of this entire situation.

"Tell us about the security force on the island. How do we beat it?", Maddox asked.

"In the dossier you have a complete blueprint of the island, including the facility layout. See those red Xs on the blueprint?", Bill asked.

The team nodded in confirmation.

"Those X's are the approximate locations of security guard towers and various security posts on the island," Billy explained.

"There's a large cluster of buildings on the North East

156

side of the island. What is that?", Jason asked.

"That? Oh, that's nothing. That's an abandoned facility. It's an old Fort. Don't worry about that. The main facility is located on the West side of the island. It is imperative that you land on the West side of the island," Billy explained.

"I mean, I'd be a fool not to ask. Why does that matter where we make landfall?", Dirk asked.

"The East side of the Island has uncontrollable storm swells at night. You'll capsize and die. That's why. The West side is the only vector of approach that doesn't result in your death, but will result in a plausible rescue scenario," Billy explained.

"Okay. How do we get there?", Jason asked.

"Well, we're at a marina, full of fishing boats. Use your imagination? I don't know. Be creative," Billy explained.

"You expect us to ship out from here?", Jason asked.

"That's why I'm paying top dollar. Flip to the final page of the dossier," Billy explained.

The team scurried to the back page of the dossier like a bunch of kids skipping pages to see how a book ended.

"Each of you will be paid the sum of $150,000, in cash, for successful completion of tonight's mission. That includes some additional Hazard pay, as needed," Billy explained.

"What if we get compromised?", Jason asked.

"I'm paying you not to get compromised," Billy replied.

"Yeah, but what if we do?", Dirk asked.

"I know, I know, I know. This is a lot to think about. But, this is rush order and I was told you were the best low budget operators this side of the Eastern Seaboard. How about you guys think it over. I'll need an answer by, let's say, I don't know, ten minutes from now," Billy explained while looking down at his wrist watch.

"Well, if you don't mind then. I'd like to discuss it with my compatriots," Maddox said while walking away.

Billy smiled and started walking backwards towards his SUV. From what the team could tell he was just content stirring up small talk with his body guards while they thought over the proposition. The trio circled up the best they could and whispered among themselves about the mission.

"Boss, I don't like it," Jason said.

Dirk looked at Jason like he must've been crazy to pass this up. As far as Dirk was concerned this was a lottery ticket.

"Jason are you fucking high? We're talking about a lot of money here," Dirk explained.

Maddox didn't want to interject to quickly into the conversation. Maddox always let Dirk and Jason air out their feelings before stepping in to make a decision.

"Boss, we need this. I need this," Dirk explained desperately.

"Why would this guy shell out $450,000 to complete strangers?", Jason asked.

"The U.S. Government spends around 600 Billion Dollars a year on Defense related spending. Whatever he is paying us, it's a drop in the bucket compared to the amount of money he stands to make re-upping the security contract for the island," Dirk explained.

Jason moaned and groaned for a second only to be broken by Maddox.

"Jason, is it doable?", Maddox asked.

Jason took a second to stroke his beard, one of his more rugged and charming features. His beard was oiled like a well-tuned classic muscle car getting prepped for an auction.

"Doable… yes. Advisable, no," Jason explained.

"All I'm asking is how. How would you do it?", Maddox asked.

Jason started rubbing the top of his head to ponder the question like a bowler polishing a bowling ball. Jason had a perfectly round and shiny bald head. The fading sunlight beamed a yellow tint from his forehead. Sweat droplets began to form around the hinges of his sunglasses. Jason was one of the most patient marksmen in the world, he once held a sniper's nest for *Five* days waiting for a target to come out of his compound. Jason excelled at soldiering and long-range combat, but where he really excelled was during the planning phase of a mission. His approach was always methodical and Maddox appreciated that level of stewardship.

"*If* we had to do it. We steal one of these fishing boats, preferably one of the boats that has a decent *Global Positioning System*. Visibility is going to be a problem and we don't want to get turned around in this mess. One wrong turn could capsize this boat and put us up stream without a canoe. We pack up small arms nothing heavy. We'll have to conceal everything in our wetsuits, which is not going to be easy. I'm thinking maybe some *9mm* sissy pistols and one or two Tranquilizer guns. Packing light is the only way to avoid suspicion. We can take out some of the lone guards and acquire their munitions as we go further and further into the facility," Jason explained.

"See, there we go. No problem!", Dirk said.

"Breaching the facility will be the easy part, Dirk. The real challenge, with our boat capsized, is how the in fuck do we get home?", Jason said.

Both men looked at Maddox for an answer. Maddox was

fixing on a possible solution like an octopus trying to open a sea shell.

"I've got that covered," Maddox said.

"What the fuck does that mean?", Jason asked.

"It's easy. We'll steal the boat from the Coast Guard," Maddox explained.

The trio of mercenaries burst out laughing in unison. The mercenaries figured this was an elegant solution to a complex problem.

"Jason, if you're not okay with this. Let's just walk…", Maddox said.

Jason thought it over, looked at Dirk, looked at Maddox and begrudgingly started nodding his head. What followed was a brief moment of moans, grunts and sighs.

"Fuck it… I'm in," Jason capitulated.

Maddox put his to fingers in his mouth and made a walloping whistle to get Billy's attention. They started walking towards each other and stopped about six-feet part.

"Well…? What's the verdict?", Billy said.

"We're in," Maddox said on behalf of the crew.

"I knew I could count on you," Billy replied
bombastically.

Billy snapped his fingers and one of his goons came
running over with a briefcase in hand.

"Just… one more thing…", Billy said as he handed the
briefcase over to Maddox.

"And that is?", Maddox said while opening the case.
Jason looked over as the case opened and started
laughing at the contents.

"Here it comes," Jason said to Dirk.

"All you can bring is this one Tranquilizer gun and
plastic knives," Billy explained.

Maddox shook his head in disbelief and said, "Sorry.
Did you say a single Tranq gun?"

Jason interrupted and asked, "Sorry, did you say plastic

knifes?"

"Well, yeah, but they're hard plastic…"

"Ha!"

"Part of our updated security is a new state-of-the-art metal detection system. This Tranquilizer gun is plastic and pump action. No metal. No gunpowder. In theory, you should be just fine passing through security," Billy rationalized to the group.

Dirk took off his baseball cap and ran his fingers through his long wavy hair. He was quick on the draw, kind of a cowboy, yet even he had his misgivings about this mission. Dirk tied back his pony tail. He put the cap back on and tucked the pony tail in the rear opening of his ball cap. His nervousness caught Maddox's eye. Maddox was getting the feeling Dirk was gung-ho, but was starting to get a case of buyer's remorse. Jason started spitting his chew on the ground and made a subtle groaning sound.

"I entrust we all made the right decision," Billy said almost questioningly with a downward inflection. Through and through Billy was a sleezy salesman masquerading in a three-piece suit. Billy looked at each of Mercenaries for confirmation that the job was still on. Followed by him abruptly shutting the briefcase and handing it over to Maddox.

Billy had his arm almost fully extended dangling the briefcase in front of Maddox. Maddox stared at the briefcase with this intense glare. Maddox was solely fixated on the briefcase like stock broker staring at a bag of cocaine. The briefcase represented a hell of a lot more to Maddox than just accepting a job. This briefcase was a down payment on a house, this briefcase was a new ex-wife, this briefcase was a fresh start.

The briefcase started to tremble in Billy's outstretched stubby excuse of an arm. Billy clearly hadn't exercised in sometime and as the briefcase shook his face began to turn red like a vine ripened Roma tomato. Billy clinched onto the briefcase and started to lower it. Just as it began to fall Maddox stepped in and clamped on to the briefcase with both hands.

Maddox stuck out a hand to shake on the deal. Billy smiled and latched on to Maddox's hand to acquiesce. Billy had small girly hands, just like Maddox. Maddox noticed almost immediately how clammy Billy's hands were, it was almost like clasping onto a dead fish. Maddox tried to remain as externally professional as possible and keep up a good poker face. No matter how uncomfortable the handshake. No matter how uncomfortable the meeting place. No matter how challenging the job looked on paper. Maddox was determined to knock this one out of the park and make a cool six-figure payday for the crew.

"Well, that's all well and great. You came here looking for trouble, and you got more than you bargained for. Does that sum it all up?", the Sergeant said furiously while pointing his rifle in the Mercenaries' face.

The Sergeant started pacing the room with his hands on his hips. His breathing became increasingly audible and more erratic with each passing moment. His eyes had this fire and brimstone kind of intensity to them. His face became noticeably redder as he stared at Maddox. Sergeant Allen was waiting for some kind of explanation from the Mercenary. Maddox hobbled up from the ground and propped up against the wall. Maddox's inattention or apathy only further enraged the Sergeant. He grabbed Corporal Barnes' ballistic helmet off the ground and shoved it into Maddox's chest. The helmet sloshed with blood, guts and brain matter.

"Listen here sweetheart! None of what you told me explains why the *FUCK* one of my men is splattered across the room like a bunch of *FUCKING HAMBURGER MEAT!*", the Sergeant screamed at

Maddox and repeatedly slammed his fist against the wall. Each punch left a bloodied imprint of the Sergeant's knuckles on the wall. The thuds of the punches bellowed the hallways of the Bio Lab.

Clang. Clang. Clang.

The Sergeant abruptly stopped assaulting the wall and paused, redirecting his anger towards the mercenary. He started favoring his hand, apparently when you get in a fight with a stainless-steel wall, the wall always wins. He looked down at his hand and it was covered in blood. What the Sergeant couldn't tell is how much of that blood was his and how much was Corporal Barnes's blood. Maddox looked down at the helmet and uncontrollably vomited all over it.

"Oh, great. What's next are you going to start crying?", the Sergeant said.

D'Stefano started methodically pillaging what was left of Barnes's mangled corpse. He started with recovering any munitions. He looted his corpse with an indifferent attitude.

"Sir."

"What?!?"

"He must've encountered a sizeable force. He unloaded nearly all of his ammunition. There's shell casing all over the fucking place. This place is littered with bullet holes…"

Sergeant Allen was struck with a look of complete bewilderment. The hallway was tattooed with bullet holes and shell casing, but only the scattered pieces of Corporal Barnes remained. There were no traces of what Barnes was shooting at. He looked sharply at D'Stefano and then back again at Maddox.

"What the fuck are we up against down here? He was supposed to be guarding an empty hallway. How many other Mercenaries are down here?", he desperately pleaded with Maddox as he pointed down an empty bullet-ridden corridor.

"I…"

"Janiwosky. Hernandez. Whitaker. Lindell. D'Stefano. On me."

The remaining squad members circled up on Staff

Sergeant Allen. They stood poised and ready to roll out on a moment's notice.

"We stay in tight formation. No one goes anywhere alone until we figure out what the fuck we're up against. Copy?"

"Copy."

"Sir, yes sir."

"Roger that. Tight as a virgin on prom night."

The Staff Sergeant shook his head at the immature remark. Who else but Hernandez would crack wise in a situation like this?

"As for you…", the Sergeant said and turned his focus back towards the mercenary.

Maddox was trained directly at the pool of blood surrounding what was left of Corporal Barnes. The pool was scattered about eight feet around the room. Every wall was covered with blood and brain matter like a piece of modern splatter paint art.

"Now, you can talk to me or you can talk to the Gunnery

Sergeant over there. It's up to you."

D'Stefano was fervently itching to polish his interrogation skills. He slowly pulled his combat knife from his boot for dramatic effect. He started cleaning his finger nails with the tip of his six-inch blue steel combat knife. Maddox looked unphased by the threatening gesture. Allen shook his head and patted Maddox on the shoulders with both hands. He shook his head and walked away with his back turned to Maddox. D'Stefano's expression sharply changed by the Sergeant's unspoken order. He took the Sergeant's cue as an excuse to immediately go to work. He grabbed Maddox's hair and pulled his knife up to her throat. He slid the knife slowly up towards her jugular vein. The knife made a peculiar sound as it grazed the neck skin of the mercenary. D'Stefano started using the knife to point around the room as he began to interrogate Maddox.

"You see the Sergeant over there?", he said while pointing with the knife. He began to tap the flat end of the knife on Maddox's forehead. The tapping made a feint squishy thud as the cold blade smacked the mercenaries' olive oil skin.

172

Tap. Tap. Tap.

"He's a by-the-book kind of guy. Me on the other hand. I'm a fuck-the-book kind of guy. I'm going to ask you something. I'm going to ask you one time. Do you understand me?"

Maddox looked up at the Gunnery Sergeant with her big blue eyes.

"Nod your head once if you understand me," he said with the knife pressed up against Maddox's throat.

Maddox slowly and cautiously nodded in affirmation.

"How many mercenaries are we up against?"

Maddox remained silent. D'Stefano applied more pressure to the knife. Her skin began to turn pale.

"It was just the three of us," she replied somewhat cooperatively.

"Ah. *See.* That wasn't so hard, was it? Don't feel too bad. Even the toughest hombres crack with a knife pressed up against their throat."

D'Stefano smiled, twirled his knife and shoved it back

173

into his boot's sheath.

"Now, please explain what the fuck happened down here?"

"We took a job…"

The squadron of men looked around at each other in a somewhat confused manner. The men couldn't figure out what kind of morons would try to infiltrate a Bio Weapons Lab during a hurricane?

"You took the job. Sweety. We heard that part of the story. So, then what happened?"

"We… borrowed one of the fishing boats in the marina."

"Borrowed? Let's cut the bullshit. Shall we? You fucking stole it," Hernandez interrupted.

"If you don't mind. We are somewhat pressed for time. Let's cut with the pleasantries and semantics," Sergeant Allen interjected.

"Okay, okay. You stole the boat. Then what happened?", D'Stefano asked while beginning to light up a cigarette.

"Do you mind if I have some water?", Maddox asked.

"Water? Oh, sure. I'm sorry. Are the accommodations not up to your standards? Can we get you a steak dinner and a reach-a-round?", Hernandez said jokingly.

Sergeant Allen snapped his fingers at Hernandez and pointed to his near empty cantina.

"Yes, sir. Anything you want sir. I'm here to serve," he said and threw his cantina over to Sergeant Allen.

Sergeant Allen snatched the cantina out of the air and walked over to the mercenary. He outstretched his arm and extended the cantina to the thirsty mercenary. Maddox and Allen locked eyes, she grabbed the cantina from Allen. Or, at least she tried. But, he didn't let go.

"What happened?", he asked.

Just as Maddox was about to utter an explanation. A rustling down the hallway caught the attention of the duo. Simultaneously the remaining squad turned towards the threat with guns ready to meet any kind of resistance. The men beamed LED lights down the hallway for a more thorough examination. The corridor was lit up with a florescent blue, but to everyone's dismay it was just a couple rats scurrying down the hall.

175

"What happened?", Maddox said as she slowly stood from her seated position.

Allen sharply turned back to Maddox still with his gun drawn. The adrenalin started to subside and he lowered his guard. Maddox instinctively put up her hands, not defensively but to block the LED light that was pointed right in her face.

"Would you mind? It's true what they say about you RECON guys, huh?"

"Yeah, what's that?"

"You guys are a bunch of fucking adrenalin junkies with itchy trigger fingers."

"If you have an itch that you need me to scratch, all you got to do is ask sweety," Hernandez said.

"Check that shit Hernandez," D'Stefano said kindly to his comrade.

"As you were saying…"

"Well, we commandeered the fishing boat and strategically crashed landed on the west coast of the

176

island."

"How'd you manage to pull that off?", D'Stefano
inquired.

"Didn't the Coast Guard intervene?", Hernandez asked.

"From the channel side, there is a considerable amount
of lee weigh. Fishing boats get a considerable amount of
slack, trust, especially with severe weather conditions.
Once we actually hit the island, the Coast Guard loses
jurisdiction and the island security takes over."

"Simple as that?", Allen asked.

"Meh. Basically. Yeah," she said and took a long swig
of water from the cantina.

Maddox slowly emptied out the cantina and went so far
as to hold it up above her head to let the remaining
droplets pour into her mouth.

"We scuddled the boat off the western shore of the
island. Not exactly how we planned it, but it worked. We
came in, just the three of us. Disguised as fishermen.
The island security took ten minutes to respond to the
scene, at which point we had plenty of time to fake our

injuries," she explained.

"Ah."

Maddox leaned against the wall to take a breather. The wall was rolled steel and ice cold to the touch.

"Like I said, we washed up on shore. Waited for about ten minutes until we were greeted by two goons from the Private Security company."

"Two guards? That's it? For the whole island?"

"Yup."

"The island operates on a skeleton crew over the weekend."

"Lovely."

"Go-on."

"The guards rushed down the beach to the scene of the crash. Like I said, they were run of the mill security goons. Head to toe boy scouts, like G.I. Joe over there," she said as she pointed to Janiwosky.

"You still haven't told me dick. How many other Mercs

are on the island? What kind of resistance are we dealing with?", D'Stefano further inquired.

"… They… aren't Mercs, not anymore."

"Anymore? What the fuck is that supposed to mean?", Hernandez asked.

"Hernandez shut-the-fuck-up and let the lady explain. Please, go-on.", D'Stefano said in a pleasant tone of voice.

"The security team loaded us up on their pick-up and we headed to the island Med Bay. Everything was running as smooth as a baby's bottom.", she explained.

"Just like that? No questions? No level of scrutiny? They took your situation at face value?", D'Stefano asked.

Maddox scoffed and asked, "When you got here. How was the visibility?"

"It was shit. We couldn't see past our dicks.", he replied.

"Well, I can tell you one thing. It was a lot fucking worse when we made our crash landing.", she said.

"I guess the guards figured you'd have to be pretty

fucking stupid to try a night landing on a small island during a hurricane.", D'Stefano said.

"That would seem to be the case," she replied softly.

The mercenary shifted to alleviate some of her physical discomfort. She paused for a moment to scan the room and get a good idea of what was going on.

"Everything was going according to plan, until..."

"Until, what?", D'Stefano asked in a soft tone to match the Mercenary.

"One of the Security Guards... Something Dirk said, or something he did, I don't know, the guard made us. Dirk popped off..."

"Sweetheart. Let's dispense with the cute euphemisms. Shall we?", D'Stefano repeated his earlier request in a somewhat more forceful tone of voice.

"He killed both of the Guards during transport. During the struggle the Pick-up Truck crashed into one of the back-up generators."

"You want us to believe the three of you invaded Plum

Island? Just the three of you?", Janiwosky broke his silence and interceded into the conversation.

"Believe whatever you want. That's what happened," she said resolutely.

"You see what's left of my friend over there on the ground?", Hernandez asked while approaching the mercenary from the side. Hernandez grabbed Maddox by the back of the neck and shoved her face into the fermenting mess that was Corporal Barnes' mangled rotting corpse.

"I once saw this man clear an entire house full of insurgents by himself. Single-fucking-handedly. He took two bullets and a knife to the back during the process. And you want me to believe a couple of Mercenaries or some rent-a-cop on steroids did this to him?"

Hernandez grabbed her by the vest and shoved her up against the wall. The back of her helmet cracked against wall and made a loud thud that echoed down the corridor.

"We were sold a bag of goods. These guards were anything but rent-a-cops. One of the guards recognized

Dirk's hand tattoo. Marine Raider Regiment...", she explained while conjuring some strength to resist the uncomfortable grip of Hernandez.

Hernandez looked at Maddox with a disjointed gaze. His curiosity got the better of his rage and as his fury subsided he slowly loosened his grip. He cautiously released Maddox from his vice grip and she fell to the ground like a toddle dropping her rag doll.

"We hijacked the transport and swapped gear with security guards. We still had the element of surprise and the power was running on back-up generators. Dirk was... rather relentless."

The mercenary was sitting a puddle of blood, almost completely devoid of emotion. Her face told a horrible story that her voice could barely utter. She was running on empty. She was running on fumes. She was running on nothing but adrenaline.

"This Dirk guy sounds like a real winner," D'Stefano said while looking over to the squad.

Just as Maddox was about to chime in to defend her fallen colleague a garbled transmission flared the radio waves.

"Al-pha-te-am... thi-sss-iss..."

The transmission was abruptly overtaken by a flurry of static. Hernandez started fiddling around with the radio. He stubbornly adjusted the radio dial in some desperate attempt to reach the other squadron.

"Bravo Team, repeat transmission. Bravo team, come in."

Hernandez's attempts failed to receive anything more than static.

"We got nothing, sir. The Comms are tits up."

"Maddox, I hope you can walk and chew bubble gum at the same time. Let's finish this bedtime story on the way to the generator," Sergeant Allen said.

"Sir!"

"What, Hernandez?"

Hernandez jogged up to the Sergeant's position and leaned in close.

"We have an island full of ex-special operators, guarding what, exactly? Some kind of experimental super solider serum? What the fuck is going on?"

Allen cleared his throat with a large cough. His judgment was clouded and his concentration was shot. The Sergeant took a deep breath and reclaimed his focus.

"Here's the plan. We have a job to do, people. We stay on mission. We're going to link up with Bravo Team, find Dr. Kerrigan and get that Nuclear Reactor back online."

"Sir, my vote is we get topside and radio for backup," Hernandez chimed in with his latest threat assessment.

"I mean, that sounds good to me to...", Maddox said.

Lindell squatted over the Sergeant's body and made a crucifix with his hands. He pillaged the mush and recovered the dog tags of the late Corporal Barnes.

Lindell said a somber prayer, "I am the resurrection and the life. Whoever believes in me, though he die, yet shall he live..."

Lieutenant Colonel Johnson broke his silence by firing a

184

single round of his revolver into Maddox's left foot. The unexpected shot echoed through the hallway with a ferocious CLACK. D'Stefano instinctively grabbed Johnson's gun with his right hand and slammed his fist into his jaw with his left hand. Johnson fell to the ground like a sack of potatoes being tossed off the back of a truck.

D'Stefano stood over the retired Lieutenant Colonel and said, "We don't shoot unarmed hostages, especially American hostages. Are you out of your fucking mind?"

Little did D'Stefano realize it, but he knocked the Colonel out cold. Lindell pulled out a bag of 'quick clot' from his pouch and held it with his teeth as he examined Maddox's foot.

"Hold still," he said to the moaning Mercenary.

She riled in pain and attempted to hold back the tears. Lindell noticed and remarked at the absurdity of the mercenaries' feeble effort to resist showing the pain. She took a deep breath and did her best to swallow the pain. The mercenary fought her instincts to lash out in pain. She was intent to just bury it deep down inside, like an old scarf being shoved into the back of a dresser.

"Don't be so damn macho. You got shot. Cry if you have to," Lindell said in a reassuring voice to the Mercenary.

Maddox refused to let her guard down and let out so much as a whimper escape her. Her stubbornness was a trademark, she considered it badge of honor. For a Mercenary in her profession reputation often never met reality.

Lindell gestured over to Hernandez, "See that guy over there?"

The Mercenary was unphased by his question and started taking deep lumbering breaths like a woman about to give birth to a 10-pound baby.

"Even big tough guys like Hernandez cry once in a while. Hey! Hernandez, you have a good cry lately?"

"Only after sex," Hernandez responded.

The mood noticeably lightened in the room. Everyone was dancing on the razor's edge and needed some kind of respite. Turns out a little self-deprecating humor was

186

just what the doctor ordered. Maddox smiled and started to let her guard down. Sergeant Allen on the other hand, wasn't quite sure what to do. Being indecisive was not in his nature. This situation wasn't in the handbook. This situation wasn't in the training manual. This situation wasn't what anyone had expected.

"D'Stefano relieve the retired Colonel of his weaponry," Allen ordered his team mate.

"My pleasure," he said. D'Stefano grabbed the Colonel by chest plate and forcibly cut off his tactical gear.

Mike Allen squatted down next to the Mercenary and continued the interrogation.

"Who hired you?"

She remained steadfast in her loyalty to the client. Lindell took the gauze out from his pack and held it over her foot. Allen waved him off in an attempt to get her to disclose more information.

"Who hired you?", Allen asked in a more irreverent tone. His patience was wearing thin with the Mercenary's lack of cooperation.

She cleared her throat and responded, "I told you, his name was Billy. He owned the Security Contract for the Island."

D'Stefano looked back at the Mercenary with a look of confusion on his brow.

"The Security Contractor for the Island wanted you to snatch a 70-year-old Super Solider Serum? That's your story? That's what you're going with?"

Maddox looked back at Sergeant Allen with a look of disgust and confusion.

"I guess the real question is, why in the world would Lieutenant Colonel Johnson want to shoot you?"

"How the hell should I know? You'll have to ask him."

Cough

Allen swung his rifle in the direction of the retired Colonel. Shining his rail mounted LED flashlight on the Colonel's slumbering body. He was sleeping like a baby after a good feed.

"D'Stefano. Do me a favor. Wake the Colonel up for

me," the Sergeant said with a slight chuckle.

Tony snapped his fingers twice in the direction of Lindell. Lindell pulled some smelling salts out of his back pocket and tossed them over to the Gunnery Sergeant. D'Stefano snagged the salt bags out of the air and started shaking them in his hand. He grabbed the back of the Colonel's neck and ripped the bag open in his mouth. He raised the Colonels head up slightly and muzzled his mouth. The Colonel jolted back to life in an instant. He looked around the room carefully trying to regain his composure. The Gunnery Sergeant had his knee firmly implanted into the chest of the Colonel. The squad guarded the corridor with an unparalleled zeal, that only to be matched by their own paranoia. There was a heightened sense of awareness after finding the remains of the once beloved Medical Sergeant.

"You good?", D'Stefano looked at the Lieutenant Colonel with skepticism. He could care less about the real answer, Tony was merely attempting to gauge the threat level.

"I'm good," the Lieutenant Colonel said trying to get up from the ground.

"Good. No more hooting and hollering from you and we should all be copesetic," D'Stefano said while politely restraining the Lieutenant Colonel. To his surprise, the retired Colonel was not putting up any resistance.

"Get him up on his feet," the Sergeant ordered.

Whitaker and D'Stefano grabbed the Lieutenant Colonel and lifted him up by his ears like an old cartoon.

"Okay. We're going to start over. Fresh start," the Sergeant announced and clapped his hands together.

The Intelligence Officer cleared his throat with an audible gulping sound. It was understood that the time for fucking-around was long over. It was understood that the time for withholding information was long over. It was understood that the time for friendly interrogations was long over.

"I want you to listen and listen carefully. That way you know how serious I am about this question. I want you to truly comprehend me," the Sergeant put his hands on the shoulders of the retired Colonel and then gently patted his face with both palms. The Sergeant turned around to D'Stefano and snagged the knife from his boot. He walked over to Barnes' helmet and grabbed it as well. He kicked the helmet over to the Lieutenant Colonel. It swashed back and forth with blood as it slid over to the Colonel.

"I'm going to ask you one time and one time only," he said while twirling the knife in a spherical looping motion. The Sergeant walked back over the Colonel and cut the respirator from his face. Tensions were running high and the Sergeant was trying to prevent this mission from becoming a complete boondoggle.

"If you give me some chicken shit answer, hell, if you even look at me wrong. I'm going to make you drink this shit," he said while pointing over to the Corporals blood laden helmet. The Helmet swashed with an amalgamation of brain matter and chunks of skull.

The Lieutenant Colonel let out an uncomfortable gulp, this time it was a little less audible than before. Large sweat droplets began to run down his forehead and cover the brow above his eyes. The droplets swelled up creating these comically large reservoirs of sweat. It was becoming rather obvious to the men that the Lieutenant Colonel had no actual combat experience. How that could happen is anyone's guess.

"The luxury of time is one we no longer possess. The luxury of having the element of surprise is one we no longer possess. The luxury of keeping mission critical intel to ourselves is one we no longer possess. That being said, what-the-fuck are we dealing with down here?"

The color fell from his face and he almost went limp. D'Stefano and Whitaker noticeably had to hold up the retired Colonel. To the untrained eye it looked like the Colonel was attempting to struggle, but in reality he was close to passing out.

"You know, Fort Terry was founded in 1897. My grandfather was stationed on the island around 1900. His son was stationed in 1950. And I was stationed here in 1990. The island has served one purpose all those many years. The Fort has served one purpose all those years."

Mike Allen was not amused with the story time bullshit, so he held up the helmet and tipped it towards the Colonel.

The Colonel took a deep breath and said, "Experimental

Bio Weapons. The last resort kind of Bio Weapons. World Enders. The first WMDs were developed on Plum Island."

Preach pulled out his bible to calm his nerves and read a passage aloud, *"When the Lamb broke the fourth seal, I heard the voice of the fourth living creature saying, "Come." I looked, and behold, an ashen horse; and he who sat on it had the name Death; and Hades was following with him. Authority was given to them over a fourth of the earth, to kill with sword and with famine and with pestilence and by the wild beasts of the earth."*

"When my father took over as the head chemical weapons specialist for Fort Terry, he had…"

"Had what?"

"He had to deal with some unique challenges…"

"Such as?"

"The Fort experimented on run of the mill type stuff in the beginning; lime disease, Spanish Flu, you know, things like that… That all changed around 1950."

"What happened in 1950?"

193

"Operation Paperclip, that's what happened," the Colonel said in self-assured tone.

The men all stared back at the Colonel with blank expressions. The men were understandably confused by the history lesson.

"Don't any of you kids read? Operation Paperclip? No? Nothing?"

The Colonel looked at the squadron with a superficial smile garnished with a splash of amusement.

"Berlin was split down the middle in *Forty-Seven*. The Russians took the East and we took the West. We took over 1600 Nazi Scientists, Engineers and various technicians out of Germany. We took them, gave them nice fake American names and boom we made them American citizens. All courtesy of the soon to be renamed Office of Strategic Services… the forerunner for the C.I.A…"

"Get the fuck out of here…", Hernandez said.

"Who do you think founded this very building? Gentlemen, we're standing in the epicenter of Bio

194

Weapon development for the better half of the last century. The deadliest diseases known to man, right here in this building. All thanks for Nazi scientists and gain of function research."

At this point, D'Stefano and Whitaker had retracted their grip from the Colonel. He wasn't a threat, at least, not compared to what the men might face in the inner workings of Building 257. The mission took a bizarre turn for the worse, like the moment when the crew on the Titanic realized they were about to hit an iceberg.

"The German Scientists were instrumental in the development of all sorts of viruses in this lab. They were ruthlessly efficient and exacting in their genetic sequencing. Overnight we went from playing checkers to 4D chess, it was a gamechanger in Bio Warfare. Taking non-human viruses and manipulating the genetic sequencing to make them compatible with human hosts."

"The Super Solider Serum… it was real?", Maddox proclaimed.

The squad looked back to Maddox as she stood up and dusted off her uniform. Plumes of dust exploded off the uniform she stole from the security guard. As she patted down the uniform she noticed the name badge stitched into the breast pocket. This sobered up the mercenary to the reality of her situation. People are dead and mostly that was a direct result of her actions.

"Believe it or not, it is as real as you and I. *SSS-1* was the kind of virus you tucked away and never spoke about. The initial testing wasn't... it wasn't what we expected. So, the brass scrapped the project and moved on to other research. Before I left, they were more interested in some kind of Bat research or some nonsense."

"What does it do?", Janiwosky asked.

"The real question isn't what does it do. No, no, no. The real question is, how do you survive an outbreak?"

"So, what're you saying? Barnes was attacked by some kind of Super Solider?"

"Could be. Or, it could be a bunch of Mercenaries running around tearing up the place. What I'm saying is that, I don't know," the Colonel said indigently. He attempted to get into a more comfortable position, but was only met with Whitaker shaking his head. The Colonel realized he was out of friends. The Colonel realized he had made his bed. The Colonel realized he needed to spill the beans.

"God help us if this is SSS-1..."

"How about we keep God out of this one?", Lindell added to the conversation.

The retired Colonel let out a large sigh of relief and continued his remarks, "The SSS-1 had a 99% kill ratio in the clinical trial of infected patients."

"What happened to the other 1%?", Hernandez inquired to the Intelligence Sergeant.

"Initial testing of the virus mutated patients in a way... The virus enhanced the patients' speed, increased awareness to threats, made the soldiers into damn near unstoppable killing machines..."

"Okay, well. That's just lovely," Hernandez responded while flickering his light on and off in the face of the retired Colonel.

"How does this shit spread? Is it airborne?", Sergeant

Allen asked.

"If we're dealing with SSS-1, which is still yet to be confirmed, the good news is that it can only spread from direct injection into the blood stream. It's not airborne... At least that is the intel I have on SSS-1," the Colonel slowly trailed off into a silent stupor.

"Hey, so it's not all bad news, right?", Hernandez squawked and went back to scanning the room with his flashlight. Hernandez wasn't frightened easily, but this mission had clearly struck a nerve.

Whitaker pulled the Sergeant aside for an off-the-books conversation. The kind of conversation that wouldn't make *After Acton Report*. The kind of conversation that no operator ever wanted to have. The kind of conversation that created vendettas.

"Sarge, I've got a bad feeling about this guy."

"What do you suggest I do about it, exactly?"

Whitaker looked back at the Lieutenant Colonel for a moment. The Colonel stared at the ground with a lifeless and bland expression. Whitaker pulled the Sergeant in close with his hand over his shoulder. He was doing his best to keep the topic of this conversation between the two men.

"He's going to get us all killed, sir. Look at him. He's a company man. He's been withholding mission critical information from us this whole time. What more does he have to do?"

The Sergeant attempted to sneak a look back at the Lieutenant Colonel, like a guy sneakily checking out an attractive girl at a bar without making it too obvious.

The Sergeant covered his mouth and said, "I-I can't."

"The men trust your judgment. The men will follow you to hell and back. This piece of shit will be our undoing. He'll stab us in the back the first chance he gets."

Ordinarily Whitaker was the most cocksure of the bunch, but for some reason was reticent with this sidebar conversation. Mike wooed Whitaker into a more candid conversation.

"What're you saying? Be concise about what you say next. Don't sugar coat it."

"I'm saying I care about you. I'm saying I care about this squad. I'm saying I could care less about this motherfucker. I'm saying maybe, maybe he was hit by a stray bullet. Or, maybe we lock him in a broom closet. The longer he tags along with us, the more time for him to scheme our demise."

The Sergeant stared at Whitaker with an unpleased expression stamped across his face. Whitaker was laying an impassable conundrum at his feet. The Sergeant relied on Whitakers unshakable judgment in the past and it ended up saving his life more than once. He took a deep breath and slowly exhaled. It was a lame attempt to stall for time as he mulled over Whitaker's proposition.

"He's not one of us," Whitaker pleaded.

"You're right. But, he's our responsibility," the Sergeant replied dismissively.

"Sir…"

"Those are your orders, Todd," the Sergeant placed his hand on Whitakers left shoulder and said loud enough for the entire squad to take notice.

The Sergeant tolerated some healthy back and forth. The Sergeant tolerated some heathy discussion. The Sergeant tolerated hearing each man's point of view. What the Sergeant didn't tolerate was insubordination.

"Sir, yes sir," Whitaker said and immediately halted his protest.

"Janiwosky please detain the *retired* Lieutenant Colonel."

Kyle didn't pack any restraints for this mission. Taking prisoners wasn't very customary for this squad. He rummaged through his backpack looking to rig up some kind of solution.

"Ah! That'll do the trick," he said aloud while pulling out some rappelling cord from his bag.

"You know what you're doing son? I'm your superior officer," the Colonel said as Janiwosky began to bind his hands behind his back.

"Sure do!", the Corporal said while tightening the Colonel's restraints.

"Anything else we can do for your Colonel? Maybe a

Mai Tai and a blowy?", Hernandez asked while shaking his head in disbelief. Hernandez was unpleased by the lack of intelligence coming from the intelligence officer.

"On me," Allen ordered the squad.

The Squadron hastily diverged to the Sergeant's position. They formed a small cluster around the Sergeants position. The Sergeant took a knee and started mapping out a plan for the squad. One thing the men knew about Mike Allen and it was that he always relished the planning process.

"What's the plan, boss?", D'Stefano asked with genuine curiosity.

The men eagerly awaited their marching orders. Each one of them was ready, able and willing to spill blood for their fallen comrade. At the drop of a hat, the men were prepared to vanquish any foe and any threat that lay in wait. It was time for some 'get back'.

"What do we know?", Allen polled his Squad for an answer. Back in the real world, Mike Allen was a big shot business tycoon at some insurance company. He always found it useful to pretend to get people involved in the decision-making process.

"Well, this building is about to collapse in on us like a falling house of cards."

"And?", Mike asked.

"And, Bravo Team is MIA somewhere in the facility."

"And, what else?", Mike asked.

"Barnes is KIA."

"And?", Mike asked.

"Whereabouts of Dr. Kerrigan are still unknown."

"Exactly. We don't know dick. Right?", the Sergeant reassured the group of their strategic implied odds. The men clutched onto their M4's like a bunch of old ladies clutching onto their purses in a bad part of town. The men casually shook their heads in agreement as Mike paraded them through a crash course in the Democratic Leadership Style.

"But, you know who does?", the Sergeant said as he put a spot light on Maddox and Colonel Johnson.

"*These two vagabonds*," the Sergeant said while pointing at the Mercenary and the Colonel. In an instantaneous sign of solidarity the squad started nodding in agreement.

"These *two* dumb bastards are how we make it out of here alive. These two are the proverbial keys to the kingdom. These two are how we salvage this op," the Sergeant repeated.

Maddox stood up from her prone position and outstretched her hands. She clasped them together and cracked all of her knuckles at once. She finally found enough freedom to engage with the squad.

"Well boys, I'm game. One thing though, if I'm going down this Rabbit Hole with you. I'll need some firepower," the Mercenary explained to her new squad mates.

D'Stefano grinned and detached one of his sidearm's from its holster. He wasn't very fond of his 45-caliber nickel-plated hand-cannon, but it would be in fine hands with the Mercenary. He wiped some blood off the gun and handed it over to the Mercenary.

"That settles that. D'Stefano takes point and lets GTFO," Mike ordered the squad.

"Sir, yes sir," D'Stefano said and turned down the corridor with his barrel drawn.

"Followed by Janiwosky on his hip," he further ordered his team.

Janiwosky shot a thumbs up and moved into position behind D'Stefano.

"Lindell, please do us all the favor of escorting the Colonel."

"With pleasure," he said while grabbing the Colonel's arm. Lindell's grip clamped onto the Colonel like a piece of wood between a vice grip.

"Maddox you're by my side at all times. If Maddox dies, we all can kiss our asses goodbye."

"Yeah, I like the sound of that. Keep me alive at all costs, boys," she said with a smile and a nod. She slightly raised the 45-caliber revolver and positioned herself to moveout with the squad.

"Any questions?", Mike asked the room.

"Sir, no sir," the group shouted in unison.

The squad was subtlety swaying forward and backwards. Lindell started a feint humming. It reverberated throughout the silent hallways.

"What's the good word, Preach?", Hernandez asked.

Preach smiled and said, "*You are my hiding place; you will protect me from trouble and surround me with songs of deliverance. I will instruct you and teach you in the way you should go; I will counsel you with my loving eye on you.*"

"*Hoo-rah!* Let's move out," Mike shouted over the comm line.

D'Stefano started walking down the hallway with his gun drawn. He swiveled his barrel from the left to the right of the hallway. He was making sure that no crevasse was unchecked. He was ready for some real carnage. He was ready for some get back. He was ready to get revenge for his fallen comrade in arms. Each footstep that the squad took echoed on the tile floor. The pitter pattered of the rain was still lingering in the background. The floor tiles were clearly neglected and poorly maintained over the years. The squad followed D'Stefano's lead down a long corridor. The corridor was long, narrow and tall. At the end of the hallway there was an emergency Exit sign flickering on and off. D'Stefano noticeably slowed his pace to a crawl, like a car puttering along on its last ounce of gasoline. He stopped at the end of the hallway and started to examine the door with a pocket LED flashlight.

"Sir. Seems we've located the main stairwell."

"No shit Sherlock."

"Keep digging Watson."

"Zip it," the Sergeant whimpered as he stepped up to the door. He began to evaluate the integrity of the door. He pressed up on the door with his forearm. Unfortunately, life wasn't going to be that easy for the Sergeant, because it didn't budge an inch. He turned to Whitaker and pointed his finger at him. Whitaker pulled out a wrecking bar from his backpack and stepped up to the door. He stood at the door and looked for a prime spot to pry open the door. He slammed the wrecking bar into the door. The clashing of metal on metal made a loud screeching sound. Whitaker looked back at the squad with a curious grin, like Babe Ruth stepping up to the plate at Yankee Stadium.

"Grip it and rip it," Janiwosky shouted.

Whitaker pulled back on the bar with all of his force. He groaned and moaned as he pulled back on the wrecking bar. The door snapped open and swung off its hinges. The metal slamming against the ground echoed throughout the hallway. The men stood at the ready and encircled the entrance of the stairwell.

"Janiwosky, flare."

Janiwosky grabbed a flare from Whitaker's outstretched hand. He ripped the cap off and popped the flare over his knee. He crept towards the entrance of the stairwell and with the flick of a wrist, gingerly tossed the flare down. The flare tumbled and twirled down the empty stairwell, bouncing off rails and steps. As the Corporal was about to peer his head into the stairwell, the Gunnery Sergeant grabbed his right shoulder. The Corporal's progress was instantly halted, leaving him standing in the middle of the doorway.

"Move aside, junior. I got this."

The Corporal looked back and answered the Gunnery Sergeant with a simple response. He nodded his head once and fell back. D'Stefano tilted his M4 into the upper corner of the door and then swept the upper stairwell. He pivoted to his left and looked down the stairwell. The Gunnery Sergeant looked straight forward and helped up his fist.

"Coast is clear," he said as he stepped through the doorway.

He took a long step into the stairwell and began to scan the environment in every direction. Sergeant Allen patted Janiwosky on the shoulder and pointed forward. Janiwosky plunged into the stairwell behind D'Stefano. Lindell grabbed his dog tags and nervously rubbed them together. There was a feint click each time the aluminum dog tags rubbed together. Sergeant Allen motioned over to Lindell. Lindell dropped his dog tags and moved forward into the breach. Maddox stepped up to the First

Sergeant's position. She swayed herself back and forth, leaning in and leaning out. She held the muzzle of her gun at the floor with her gaze attuned at the breach. The Sergeant smiled with an eager anticipation. He was chomping at the bit to see the 'Mad Dog' in action. He patted her on the shoulder and she breached the doorway. The rest of the squad followed D'Stefano down the stairwell. Lindell held up the rear and escorted the Colonel down the stairwell. Lindell unconsciously found himself periodically nudging the Colonel with the barrel of his gun. The squad followed the bright glare of the glowstick down the stairwell. As they proceeded down the stairwell, Hernandez slipped and his knee buckled, slamming against the wall of the stairwell.

"Fuck. Give me some light over here," Hernandez shouted while trying to recover his footing and regain his composure.

Janiwosky shined his light towards Hernandez. Hernandez looked down at the ground and grabbed onto the rail to pull himself up. The handrail was ice cold like a flag pole in a snow storm.

"What-the-fuck?!?!?!"

Hernandez held up his hand into the air and began to inspect it. His hand was crimson red, like a child who just discovered the joy of finger painting. Lindell immediately ran over to Hernandez and started assessing the scene. He grabbed his hand and started checking it.

"Where does it hurt?"

To Lindell's surprise, Hernandez ripped his hand from the grip of Medic.

"It's not mine," he shouted back at Lindell as he regained his footing.

The men started examining the stairwell in greater detail. Blood had soaked every inch of the stairwell. The question was, whose blood was it? Mike Allen squatted at the bottom of the stairwell and grabbed the flare from the floor. He waved it in the air in an attempt to brighten the room. The blood had a darker hue than the blood found upstairs. There were large black chunks of congealed blood and guts sprinkled across the floor. The mood in the room shifted to a more morose and somber feeling. The pool of blood had foot prints leading to the entrance of main biolab. The men were in hot pursuit of something. Spent shell casings littered the ground floor of the stairwell. Whitaker knelt down like a catcher behind home plate.

"Looks like we have some 5.56mm, 223, 45 and even some 9mm scattered around here sir…", he said while examining the scene.

"Looks like there was gun fire in damn near every direction…", he explained.

Whitaker pointed his flashlight upward to find bullet holes everywhere, even in the ceiling.

"In every direction…", he repeated while shining light on the ceiling.

D'Stefano scrutinized the handle of the door like a scientist looking through a microscope. He stared at the handle of the door with an intense frustration. At first glance, it seemed completely normal. For some reason that perturbed the Gunnery Sergeant.

"Sir,"

Allen slung his rifle over his shoulder and proceeded to the Gunnery Sergeant's position.

"How we looking Gunny?"

"It looks clear,"

The Sergeant walked back to the former intelligence sergeant. His boots made squishy thuds stomping around in the blood. He walked up to the retired Colonel and politely pleaded, "So… Anything you want to add before we breach that door?"

"Janiwosky get up here and help me with the door," the Gunnery Sergeant shouted to the young Corporal.

The Corporal hustled up to the door and pulled out two wrecking bars from his backpack. D'Stefano held up his hand and Janiwosky tossed him one of the wrecking bars. The two men plunged their respective wrecking bars into the door jam.

"On 3," he said while holding up three fingers.

Janiwosky nodded in accordance with the Gunny's request.

"1…2…3!", he said as both men leaned back and mustered the strength to pry the door open. Both men were outstretched as far as the bar could bend. The wrecking bars simultaneously snapped like a mad dog snarling at a mailperson. The two operators looked at each other with a certain level of astonishment and pride. The rest of the team found it an opportune time to heckle, hoot and holler.

215

"Now what?", D'Stefano asked.

"Breacher rounds?", Janiwosky asked.

"Breacher rounds," Whitaker said gleefully.

Whitaker smiled and pulled out a box of experimental titanium breacher rounds from his backpack. The Sergeant ejected his magazine and Whitaker handed over the box of ammunition. He loaded up the magazine with the experimental rounds. It wasn't often that the Sergeant got to experiment with new weapons. He was as giddy as pothead eating a box of Girl Scout cookies outside of a Medical Marijuana dispensary. The Sergeant slammed the magazine into the rifle and pulled back on the charging handle. He handed the rifle over to Whitaker to breach the door. Whitaker held the rifle waist level and shot from the hip.

"Okay, boys. Let's see what these things are made of," he said and blasted the door.

Clack! Clack! Clack! Clack!

Whitaker suspended his barrage and handed the rifle back to the Sergeant. The Sergeant grabbed the rifle

back from Whitaker and slung it back over his shoulder.
He pointed both of his fingers up and then at the door.
D'Stefano and Janiwosky both charged the door like
linebackers going after a quarterback. The door snapped
off the hinges and flung into the next room. Janiwosky
lost his footing and the door took him into the next
room, like a kid riding a newly wetted slip and slide.
D'Stefano stumbled to the ground face planted into the
fresh pool of blood. Lindell immediately raised his
weapon to put some light on the entrance to the bio lab.
To his great surprise the facility was immaculate inside.
The men were shocked by the nearly pristine and
unmolested Bio Lab.

D'Stefano cautiously crept into the cavernous room. He
carefully scanned the room, making sure to step over
Janiwosky in the process. D'Stefano was feeling
charitable and kneeled down to the Corporal and picked
him up off the ground. D'Stefano glanced back at the
stairwell and motioned over to the squad.

"Coast is clear,"

The squad quickly infiltrated the unoccupied the Bio
Lab. Mike instinctively grabbed some glowsticks from

217

his backpack and started scattering them about the empty bio lab. The men scanned the room for some kind of clue. Janiwosky picked up on a feint trail of blood-stained foot prints. The trail led to a pile of manila file folders scattered across the laboratory floor. The white porcelain tile floor shined the green glow from the glowsticks. Janiwosky squatted down to peruse the file folders. As Janiwosky was thumbing through the file folders, he couldn't help but wonder what happened.

"Find anything?", Allen inquired.

"Whatever they were looking for in this mess, they sure ended up leaving in a hurry, sir,"

Janiwosky seditiously started tossing aside folder after folder, like a monkey discarding a banana peel.

"Ah! Bingo! Here we go boys," he said.

Janiwosky found the proverbial needle in the haystack. He held up a folder with a big fat red "Confidential" stamped across the outer folder jacket. There was a broken red plastic seal that once contained the folder. The plastic seal was covered in bloody fingerprints. The Corporal tossed it over to the First Sergeant for further inspection.

"What do we *have* here?", the First Sergeant asked while auditing the folder.

The Sergeant's casual review of the folder turned to chthonic with each proceeding flip of the page. The Sergeant closed the file folder and bent it under his armpit. He began to pace back and forth, pondering his next move.

"What is it Sarge?", Whitaker impatiently implored the indigent Sergeant to inform the ignorant squad of the important intel.

The Sergeant pulled open the folder to expose a photo of the Chief Scientist responsible for Project SSS-1. It was none other than the retired Lieutenant Colonel. Whitaker stood resolute as his prior seemingly paranoic state was now thoroughly justified.

"Who else?"

"Ha!", Hernandez started laughing out loud.

"I can explain…", the Colonel pathetically pleaded with the pissed off squad.

"Says here… that not only did you head the research project for SSS-1, you were working on gain of function research. To… to make it more transmissible to humans."

"Well, yes… But…"

While the rest of the squad was bickering, D'Stefano was looking over the trail of bloody footprints. He was fixated on the crimson boot prints. He'd seen it before somewhere, but couldn't immediately recall where. The wheels were churning in the Gunnery Sergeant's head for some kind of remembrance.

"I recognize these boots…", he said slowly.

D'Stefano popped up from his squatted position and started looking for more clues. D'Stefano started searching out the remainder of the floor. He wasn't sure what he was looking for, but he felt he was hot on a trail of something. He was rummaging around like a Hound dog hot on the trail of a pheasant.

"Sir…"

Sergeant Allen looked over to the distraught Gunnery

Sergeant. The Gunnery Sergeant roamed off the beaten trail, about twenty or so feet to the corner of the laboratory. The bio lab was a labyrinth of desks, science kits and cabinets, almost like one of those cornfield mazes. The Sergeant shined a light over to the Gunny. The Gunny calmly held up a set of dog tags. He held the dog tags in the air and they dangled against the Gunny's forearm. He quickly flung them over to the Sergeant and the Sergeant snatched them out of the air.

"I recognized those boot prints, sir," the Gunny explained in a distraught tone.

The Sergeant found this claim to be somewhat outlandish, but still trusted the Gunny knew what he was talking about. Who else but the Gunnery Sergeant would comprehend that level of granular detail?

"Those are Men's Forced Entry Tactical Waterproof boots, sir," he explained.

The squad looked over at D'Stefano waiting for some further explanation. Hernandez had slung his rifle over his shoulder and rested it behind his neck. Hernandez needed to take a breather, the fatigue was beginning to take its toll on the operator.

"Speak on it, Gunny," Allen shouted.

"Standard issue boots for the NSF…", he explained.

Mike was taken aback by his discovery. He immediately clammed up and straighten his back up like the first time a nun slams a ruler on your desk in Catholic school. He looked down at the dog tags. The tags were mangled, almost like somehow had digested them.

"You're saying these dog tags belong to an NSF squad?"

"Sir, yes, sir!"

The Sergeant immediately turned to the retired Lieutenant Colonel. He stuck out the dog tags and began to berate the Colonel. He was hoping to get some kind of authentic response from the Colonel, but wasn't going to hold out for hope. The Sergeant grabbed two executive leather chairs and faced them off in the middle of the room. The Sergeant sat down in the first chair and motioned Janiwosky to delicately place the Colonel in the other. Janiwosky instinctively picked up on the Sergeant's subtle gestures.

"Colonel Johnson… you got some explaining to do…",
Mike said while pulling out a loose cigarette from his
badly damaged cigarette carton.

"I see… Is it finally time to cut the boy scout routine,
sergeant?", the Colonel asked defiantly.

The Sergeant smiled and said, "Made it all the way to
Eagle, actually."

The Sergeant took a long drag from the cigarette and
adroitly blew the plume of smoke into the face of the
Colonel. Mike wanted to make a blatant statement to the
Colonel. He wanted to Colonel to understand the futility
of withholding any further information. Time would tell
if the Colonel could read between the lines. Mike
changed his mind and skipped the subtle tactics. He
figured it was time to flip the table. He removed his M9
from his holster and placed it on the left hand of the
Colonel.

"I'm going to ask you this question one time. I'm
assuming we have enough rapport at this point in our
relationship to where you will trust me when I say,
Don't fuck with me on this."

The Colonel was tired of being paraded around the facility like a captured POW. His patience was wearing rather thin and didn't care much for the false bravado of the Sergeant.

"The thing about threatening someone with a gun Sergeant, is that the captive has to believe the interrogator is serious enough to follow through with the threat."

Without a moment of hesitation the Sergeant made a statement that he was no longer fucking around. He swiftly pulled the trigger of the M9 and put a 9MM round through the right hand of the Colonel. The Colonel screamed a piteous cry of panic and pain. Janiwosky immediately attempted to gag the Colonel and silence his hollering. Lindell dashed over to the Colonel and started dressing wounds. With a combination of quick clotting packets and a little bit of morphine the Medical Corpsman was able to sooth the Colonel.

Sergeant Allen pushed Lindell aside and looked directly into the eyes of the Colonel. The time for subtly was over. The time for courteous coddling was over. The time mucking around was over. For the first time, the Colonel saw the real Mike Allen and was petrified of Sergeant. The sentiment of the Colonel was adorned by the rest of the squad.

Whitaker started rubbing his hands together and whispered with a smirk, "Time for some get back."

"Now, where were we before you rudely interrupted me, Colonel?", Mike asked and placed the barrel of his gun on the right hand of the Colonel.

"Sir, we're shooting hostages now?", Lindell asked the Sergeant.

A glimpse of hope poured into the Colonel's eyes. Mike de-cocked the M9 and started to shake his head. He turned to Lindell and ordered him to, "Secure the hallway."

To the dismay and shock of the squad, Lindell did not budge from his position. The Sergeant stood up and bowed up on Lindell. He grabbed onto Lindell's vest and pulled him in close. The Sergeant started whispering something into Lindell's ear. The room was as silent as library, but none of the men could hear a word. Lindell shouldered his firearm and diffidently marched into the hallway.

"Sorry about that," the Sergeant said while pulling the chair in close to the Colonel.

The Colonel looked over to the rest of the squad in an attempt to find a sympathetic ally to his cause. Unfortunately for him, there would be no such luck.

"Where were we, again?", he asked in a comically sinister tone. Mike began to noticeably slow the conversation done and take strategic pauses. He found long ago that pausing was a great source of creating undue tension during an interrogation. It was something he learned working as an Insurance Salesman in the San Fernando Valley.

"Oh, yes. I had a question," Mike crossed his legs and efferently started smoking his cigarette. He took a long puff from that cigarette and stared into the eyes of the Colonel.

"Now, I'm no PHD or nothing like that. I live in the real world. I come from the school of hard knocks. But, when I see dog tags from the Coast Guards' National

Strike Force covered in blood and goo. I get to thinking," he said while tapping the ash from his cigarette on the lap of the Colonel.

"I get to thinking, maybe I wasn't apprised of all the critical, need-to-know information on this mission," he said and puffed smoke into the general direction of Colonel.

"Look…", the Colonel pleaded with Mike Allen.

"No! You look! Shut-the-fuck-up!", he shouted down the Colonel.

The Colonel obliged and sat in the chair content with remaining completely closemouthed.

"It looks to me like you sent in the NSF. It looks to me like we're the second team on site. It looks to me like we're cleaning up after your major fuck up."

The Colonel kept his composure and sat quietly in the chair. He wasn't sure how to interject himself back into the conversation without spurring the Sergeant into a fit of justified rage.

"I've got dead Marines in this building, people I would

have easily given my life for. Now is the time to come clean, once and for all," Mike Allen said while pulling out his sidearm.

He slowly pulled back on the slide to check for ammunition and cock the gun for action. He flicked the cigarette at the Colonel and it bounced off of his forehead. D'Stefano was shocked, because for the last ten years serving with Mike Allen, he had never witnessed this side of him. Mike rose from his chair and placed the M9 shoulder of the Colonel.

"Speak now or forever hold your peace," the Sergeant said while cocking back the hammer on his pistol.

"The NSF responded almost instantaneously. There's a squad on standby just off the coast of the island. We kept them on standby for this very situation," he blurted out into total capitulation.

"*See.* That wasn't so hard. Was it?", the Sergeant said while de-cocking his firearm and placing it back into his waistband.

"Dr. Kerrigan was the intelligence officer tagging along with the NSF team. She had first-hand knowledge of the island facility…"

"Okay. So, what happened?", the Sergeant asked and drooped the bloody dog tags over the head of Lieutenant Colonel Johnson.

"They infiltrated the facility and all hell broke loose. We received an *S.O.S* from Dr. Kerrigan about twenty minutes into the operation."

"You knew this whole time…", Maddox gasped.

"I had my orders, just like you," the Colonel explained.

"Which were what, exactly? To get in, get the virus and fuck us in the ass?", Hernandez shouted belligerently.

"Not exactly… We knew that a Mercenary incursion was only possible with an inside player. For years, Plum Island had to deal with leaks to the Soviets. High level leaks of classified intel. We surmised it was Dr. Kerrigan, but could never prove it. Who else could it have been for so many years?"

"Let me get this right. You suspected this 'Doctor' of espionage and then turn her around and send her in to assist as an intelligence officer for a counter-terrorism mission. In hopes to what? Catch her in the act? Catch her red handed once and for all?", Sergeant Allen blurted out hysterically in disbelief.

"I mean, when you say it like that, it sounds pretty bad," the Colonel admitted.

"D'Stefano, give me your knife. I'm going to guy this fool," Hernandez shouted as he turned to the corner of the room where D'Stefano was standing.

The Gunnery Sergeant seemed unphased by his request. Hernandez slowly raised up his tac-light in the in the direction of the Gunny.

"Tony?", he asked.

Not a word came out of the Gunnery Sergeant's mouth.

"Yo, Tony! You deaf or what?", he said while approaching the Gunny from behind.

The Gunnery Sergeant deliberately raised up his head and turned towards the Sergeant. His eyes were heavily dilated with a maroon color. Hernandez halted his ingress and asked, "You okay bud? You don't look so hot…"

D'Stefano was favoring his hand as it began to uncontrollably spasm and gush with blood. The blood spewed across the room painting the walls of the bio lab. Hernandez was flabbergasted as D'Stefano wailed in pain and floundered about the bio lab. He couldn't help but be a bystander to what could only be described as an out-of-control human sprinkler system. The strength was immediately flushed from his body. Maddox broke her trance and barreled down on the Gunnery Sergeant tackling him to the ground.

"Stand still Gunny," she said.

The rest of the squad immediately followed suit and disserted any notion of personal wellbeing as they dove on the Gunnery Sergeant. One by one the Gunnery Sergeant tossed the squad members to the side. The more the Gunny squirmed, the more the men fumbled about trying to subdue him. After several minutes of seizing and spasming the Gunnery Sergeant went completely limp. When the chaos subsided, Lindell looked over the Gunnery Sergeant's corpse for some kind of clue as to what happened. Lindell held his head to D'Stefano's heart and heard nothing but a shattering silence. He was as dead as a door nail. He decided to go right to the source and began to examine his hand. The veins on his hands were blackened and bloated beyond belief. There seemed to be a scratch of some kind at the epicenter of the hand.

"Form a perimeter," Allen shouted at the operators in an attempt to make sense of what just transpired. He took a second to catch his breath and grapple with the reality of his best friend laying lifeless on the floor.

"Lindell, figure out what happened. Janiwosky, guard the prisoner. Maddox…"

"Sir,"

"What is it?", Allen shouted.

Janiwosky pointed over to the chair where the Colonel was formerly bound. The chair was tipped over and the restraints dangled off the chair.

"Oh, you got to be fucking kidding me," the Sergeant said.

Maddox took a moment to recuperate. She wiped the blood from her face and took a few calming breaths. She got up to her feet and walked over the D'Stefano's body.

"What's the prognosis?", she asked Lindell.

"Too soon to tell," he said while examining the body.

"Hernandez! Show me where D'Stefano was standing when you found him?"

Hernandez attempted to locate the Gunny's exact position. He started scanning the room and pointed over to the general direction.

"I think he was over by that chair with the lab coat hanging on it. Yeah, he was looking over the pool of blood by the dog tags."

"Ah. Okay. Let's take a look, shall we?"

Lindell walked over to inspect the site. He wasn't sure what to look for. Something cut his hand, but it could have been anything. He squatted down and scrutinized the scene by looking over the spot with an LED flashlight. He was looking for a needle in a haystack. He squatted down to get a better look. There wasn't anything out of the ordinary as far as he could tell. Lindell grabbed onto the adjacent desk to help him stand up. As he clutched onto the desk he heard a distinctive sound followed by a piercing blow to his hand. It was the crunch of glass breaking against the skin. The Medical Corpsman grabbed his wrist to stop the bleeding, like a vice grip clamping on to a piece of wood.

"Well, I think I found what he cut his hand on," he said as he fell to his knees.

Hernandez instinctively tackled the Medical Corpsman to the ground and pulled his combat knife out from his sheath. He slammed the serrated end of the knife down on Lindell's wrist and sawed off his hand. Maddox slid over and shoved a piece of plastic in his mouth to bite down on. Lindell riled in pain and soaked the floor in an amalgamation of blood and tears.

Hernandez looked over his wrist to see if the infection had spread any further up the arm. At first glance the infection looked to be isolated to the hand. Lindell was always considered to be the lucky one of the group.

Unbeknownst to the squad, Sergeant Allen and Janiwosky had fled the laboratory to hunt down the Colonel. They tracked the Colonel like two bounty hunters hot on the trail of a recently escaped fugitive. The Mercenary grabbed a morphine syringe from the Medical Corpsman's backpack and slammed it into Lindell's chest. She speedily emptied the contents of the syringe and tossed it aside. The Corporal arched his back and waned in and out of consciousness. Maddox grabbed a packet of 'quick clot' and started pouring it over the wound. Neither Hernandez nor Maddox noticed the absence of the other two teammates.

"Elevate his legs while I figure something out," Hernandez ordered the Mercenary.

Hernandez scanned the room looking for his superior officer. In the commotion he lost his tac-light. In a spurt of quick thinking he slid over to D'Stefano and borrowed his tac-light. The way Hernandez figured it Tony wouldn't be using it anymore.

"How does it look?", Lindell asked the Mercenary.

"How does what look?", the Mercenary responded in an optimistic tone.

Lindell was barely able to muster the strength to sit up, but somehow found away unassisted by the Mercenary.

After recovering the tac-light, Hernandez started searching the room for any medical supplies.

"Bingo!", he said.

He ran over to the nearest First-Aid-Kit and ripped it clean off the wall. He took the kit under his arm like a running back who was just handed off the ball. He ran back to Lindell and flung open the kit to look for additional supplies.

"What do you need Preach? Tell me what to do, buddy."

"Take out the trauma pad and cover in that anti-bacterial ointment. We have to stop the bleeding."

Maddox yanked out the antibiotic ointment and ripped it open with teeth.

"Hold on buddy," Hernandez said while lacing the bandage in the ointment.

"This is going to hurt, so I'll need one of you to hold me down. Just in case," he said while wincing.

Maddox straddled the Medical Corpsman to pin him down. Under normal circumstances most people would find it customary for him to be stuffing dollar bills into her pockets. Under normal circumstances Hernandez would be cracking jokes. These were anything but normal circumstances. Hernandez took the dampened gauze and applied it to the lopped off wrist. The Medical Sergeant riled in pain and whimpered to the best of his ability. How Lindell remained conscious was anybody's guess at this point.

Meanwhile, in the inner corridors of the facility, Mike and Kyle had been in hot pursuit of the Lieutenant Colonel. Kyle found a trail of blood, scuff marks and smudged finger prints on one of the door handles.

"Sir...", he whispered over the Comms.

Mike turned to the Corporal's position, which was about ten feet ahead and up to the left of the Sergeant. He swung his rifle shining his rail mounted flash light in the Corporal's direction. Mike approached with delicate paces to observe the scene. He flashed a light at the door knob and took two steps back.

"Gotcha."

"What're my orders?"

"Shoot on sight. I'm done fucking around."

Janiwosky smiled and clutched on the door handle. He pulled down on the handle and muscled his way into the room. Janiwosky stumbled into the room and Mike immediately flowed in and started unloading his magazine. Janiwosky followed in kind and started blindly emptying his rounds.

Clack. Clack. Clack.

Mike cycled through his entire 30-round magazine, but was so enraged he did not realize it. Plumes of gun smoke had filled the room. Mike and Kyle simultaneously hit their mag release buttons and their magazines dropped to the floor. Mike reached into his ammo pouch and slammed in a fresh magazine, Kyle followed in tandem. Each man started laughing at their respective overzealous and premature response. The laughter immediately subsided as the men heard a nightmarish sound from behind their position.

CLICK!

It was the sound of a hammer pulling back on a gun. It was the sound of someone who had the drop on the two

238

men. It was the sound of an ambush.

"I can't let any of you leave here alive," the shadowy figure said in the background.

Janiwosky turned his head and made eye contact with the Sergeant. He had his hands raised in the air and pointed down with the tips of his finger. What followed was a barrage of gunshots in the direction of the two men, like a maelstrom of lead raining down on their position. The men turned about face and unloaded into the shadowy figure standing the hallway. Janiwosky fell to the ground, but managed to keep exchanging fire on the way down. Mike took a knee to better steady his rifle. Once more, smoke had filled the room, but this time the LED flashlights had refracted a crimson hue to the smoke. Mike took shelter behind a desk and reloaded his magazine.

"Janiwosky, you hit?"

"Sir, yes sir!", he said while patching up a stomach wound.

He did his best to conceal the wound, but the bullet ricocheted throughout his body. Blood poured out of his body like a broken slushie machine at a convenience store.

"Corporal! Cover that doorway. Buy me some time," the First Sergeant pleaded with his wounded comrade.

"Sir, yes sir,"

As the smoke started to subside the Corporal attempted to balance his rifle on his knee cap. He found it to be an impossible task given his wounds. He dropped the rifle onto the ground and it made a large thud. Sergeant Allen looked over the Corporal as the life slowly faded from his body. The Corporal mustered enough strength to pull out his sidearm and cover the doorway.

The room had cleared of any smoke, but to the dismay of the Corporal, the shadowy figure was still standing on the outer banks of the doorway. The figure held up his firearm and aimed it directly at the young Corporal. The Corporal faced down the barrel of a gun and the inevitable end to his mission.

The Corporal yelled out, "Sergeant, get down!"

Janiwosky and the shadowy figure unleashed hell on

each other. Causing bullets to scatter the room like a popcorn maker popping kernels of corn. Mike watched in awe as he reloaded his rifle with a single hand. He popped up from behind the desk and started raining bullets down at the doorway. He hobbled over to the Corporal, moving laterally from his position.

Clack. Clack. Clack.

Shots rang out like a dinner bell at supper time. Hernandez sprung up with his gun drawn and scanned the room. The light on his M4 started to flicker on and off.

CLACK. CLACK. CLACK.

Maddox dashed over to D'Stefano's body and looted his corpse for munitions. Time was of the essence. She took what she could and sprinted over to Hernandez. She slapped him on the back to break his trance.

"Hernandez. We need to move out," she said while checking her newly acquired M4.

Clack!

A single gunshot broke his hypnotic gaze. Hernandez

lowered his guard for a moment to contemplate his decisions. Whether he liked it or not, he was now in charge.

"Agreed…"

Lindell rolled on his side and pushed off the ground with his good arm. He haphazardly hopped up and leaned against the wall to stabilize his footing. He'd lost a considerable amount of blood. He'd lost a considerable amount of energy. He'd lost a considerable amount of his hands. Yet, he wasn't deterred.

"Can you fight?"

"I'm still a Marine, god damnit. Of course I can fight."

Hernandez smiled and handed his teammate a 45-Caliber *1911*. It was one of the few weapons a man could reliably load, cock and operate with one hand.

"I'll take point. Maddox you're glued to my hip. Lindell cover our six. We're going to move and move fast. I'm getting us the hell out of here," he ordered the remaining squad.

Hernandez stood silent for a moment, for the reckoning

was upon him. Lindell was drenched in his own blood, but kept a steady hand. Maddox started humming with a sense of renewed vigor. Hernandez spontaneously began to hum as well. Lindell tucked the 1911 into his armpit and pulled out his pocket bible. It was time to read one last passage, *"But stay awake at all times, praying that you may have strength to escape all these things that are going to take place, and to stand before the Son of Man."*

The Sergeant had a renewed spirt and felt a sense of replenishment. Hernandez pulled back on his charging handle and marched to the nearest exit. Sometimes you choose to lead and sometimes leadership chooses you. Hernandez plunged head first into the breach. His movements were methodical and exacting. All the years of special operation warfare had prepared him for this one moment. He remembered the advice from his first Commanding Officer, "Slow is smooth. Smooth is fast." Ten times a day, his *C.O.* had pounded that mantra into his head. The hallways were riddled with bullet holes and stank of death. He popped out a 5.56mm round from his magazine and plugged it into one of the holes, it fit like a glass slipper.

"5.56mm… All of them, by the looks of it… We're close…", he said looking down at a fresh trail of blood.

"Hold fast," Hernandez said while pointing at a slumped over body in the hallway.

The trio approached the body with a hyper-sensitive discretion. Hernandez sheepishly stepped forward and poked the corpse with the barrel of his gun. The corpse fell over and shattered into a million pieces, it scattered like marbles falling out of a marble bag.

"He's…"

"He's dead," a voice said from the shadows.

Maddox swung around and pointed her M4 at the voice.

"*Whew!* I almost damn near blew your head off. You had us worried for a second, there," she said after locking eyes on Sergeant Allen.

Allen stumbled his way out of the shadows and into the hallway. He limped over to the squad while favoring his wounds with one hand and barely holding on to his weapon.

"Where's Janiwosky?", Hernandez inquired to the lone Marine.

"He... he didn't make it," Allen explained egregiously.

"Good to see you, sir," Lindell said reassuringly.

"It's a miracle I survived," Allen explained somewhat egotistically.

"So, the Twenty-Four-Thousand-Dollar-Question is... who the fuck was that guy?"

The First Sergeant stammered over to the corpse for a closer inspection. He was nursing a bullet wound and some minor lacerations.

"Let's just see who are mystery guest is...", he said while examining the corpse. The corpse was almost completely unrecognizable. What was left of the body was loosely held together with bullet fragments.

"Maddox, grab some gauze out of my pack and help me patch up the Sergeant," Lindell recommended to the operator.

Maddox and Lindell started attending to the Sergeant's

wounds, but he barely noticed. His focus was fully engrossed on the corpse. He managed to scavenge one key piece of intel from the body. The Sergeant found a pair of dog tags under the body.

"Anthony Demarco... National Strike Force."

"Boss... What... what happened?", Hernandez asked skeptically. He couldn't fathom the possibility of going up against another Special Forces unit, let alone another American Special Forces unit on American soil.

"What happened? We walked right into an ambush. That's what happened."

Lindell knelt down to inspect the corpse.

"Sir, this man sustained over thirty gunshot wounds," Lindell said alarmingly.

"And..."

"And, and what?"

"And, it looks like some of the wounds had started to coagulate."

"I must have skipped that day biology class. What are

you saying?", Allen asked the Medical Corpsman.

"His body was trying to heal itself, sir."

"Janiwosky and I emptied three entire magazines into that son of a bitch. You're telling me what, exactly? That he wasn't dead?"

"Sir, I don't know what to think. If he was infected with that shit, I just don't know. I do know what coagulated blood looks like, and this motherfucker is covered in it," Lindell said while motioning with his hand.

"Hernandez, when was the last time we had radio contact?", Allen asked the Communications expert.

"From who? Bravo Team?"

"From anybody," Allen shouted in a sultry tone.

"Comms have been dark for the last hour, at least... or so."

"Well, fuck me sideways and call me Susie," Maddox said.

Maddox reclaimed some tactical items from the fallen solider and went about her business. Hernandez started rubbing his hands together, probably a soothing gesture to calm his nerves.

"So, we got an unknown number of operators running around here. Bravo Team is MIA. The Lieutenant Colonel is MIA or KIA. *Just* great!"

CLACK. CLACK... CLACK. CLACK.

Two gunshots rang out from both ends of the hallway. Mike and Maddox covered the North side of the hallway and Hernandez and Lindell swiveled to cover the South side of the hallway. Lindell wasn't moving like a spring chicken, but he was still deadly enough to put in some work. The squad was hunkered down into what the infamous General Erwin Rommel would call a 'kill zone'.

"Does anyone have eyes on target?"

"No, sir," Hernandez shouted.

"I don't see shit," Lindell squawked.

The dimly lit hallway was about twenty yards in each direction from the squad. The men couldn't make heads or tails of the source of the gunfire. Down the South end of the hallway, some shadowy figure scurried across from one room to the next. It went in one door and out the other, like an old episode of Benny Hill.

"Contact left!", Hernandez shouted and let out a controlled three-round burst. Lindell attempted to follow the aberration, but struggled sighting in the target. Hernandez was mindfully attempting to conserve his ammo. In the flash of an eye, the target vanished from sight. Hernandez knelt into a prone position and yelled, "Sir, one hostile. Permission to engage."

"Negative. Hold your position," he responded sharply.

The Sergeant was buying time to think, but knew every second that passed was one less second until the building collapsed. The squad patiently waited for their orders. The anticipation boiled over like pasta water frothing over a boiling pot of water.

Hernandez asked, "What's the plan Sergeant?"

The Sergeant was sitting at a fork in the road. He could go forward into the unknown or backwards back track into the unknown. Neither situation was feeling like a solid option.

"We're pressing forward."

Lindell plummeted to the ground, like a fish merchant tossing a dead fish at Seattle's famous fish market. Hernandez immediately stuck out his hand in an attempt to grab his fallen colleague.

"Sir, cover me,"

Sergeant Allen flipped around and covered the hallway as Hernandez sought to his injured comrade. Allen took a knee and pointed his rifle down the hallway with vicious intent in his heart. He was operating on adrenaline and instinct. Hernandez started looking at the Medical Corpsman's arm and the veins were pulsating with a worrisome black hue.

"Sir, the infection has started to spread…", Hernandez updated the squad.

Allen lowered his rifle and looked over at the Medical Corpsman. Lindell spat out a plash of blood laced vomit.

"Get out of here," Lindell ordered the squad while recovering to one knee. He was barely able to stabilize himself.

"Stay down," Hernandez said to no vail. Lindell pushed him aside with the little strength he could spare.

"I'm not making it out of here, but that doesn't mean you can't make it out alive."

"Don't be stupid. We can…"

"Can? Can, what? I have one fucking hand. I'm Two Hundred pounds of liability. I'll only slow you down."

"Lindell, we can…"

"Can what? Wait till I turn into that thing on the ground and then try to not let me… GO! Get out of here. I'll cover you. Let the last thing I do be worthwhile," he pleaded with the men.

The squad meandered around for a second without a word spoken amongst them. There wasn't much to say at this point. The first rule of the Marine Core is to never leave a man behind. For the first time in his storied career as a Marine, Mike was about to break that sacred oath. Mike stood up from his shooting position and abruptly walked away. Before he could take two steps Lindell grabbed his hand. Mike halted his retreat. He

251

was petrified by the heroic gesture of his comrade in arms.

"I want you to have this…", Lindell said as he handed over his pocket bible to Mike Allen.

Allen attempted to withhold his tears while Lindell started to chant his final rite of passage, *"For whoever wants to save their life will lose it, but whoever loses their life for me will save it."*

Mike begrudgingly took the bible from him and walked away. As he walked away he tapped Hernandez on the shoulder twice. Hernandez ducked down and said, "Via con dios, amigo."

He patted Lindell on the helmet turned around and followed Mike down the North end of the hallway. On his way Hernandez whispered, "Give them hell, buddy. Give them hell." Mike led point down the hallway. The sounds of potshots echoed from their rear. Lindell was slowly emptying out his magazine. As they scurried down the hallway the sounds became feinter and less noticeable. The squad advanced to the next bio lab and stopped just short of the entrance.

"Look. What waits on the other side of that door is anybody's guess. Whatever happens next..."

"Don't get poetic on us now, it doesn't fit you," the Mercenary said.

"Sir, let's do an ammo check," Hernandez said prudently.

The group acceded to the request and began to take down their weapons for an ammo check.

"I've got 30 rounds of 5.56mm and a full load in the Six-Shooter," the Mercenary said.

"Two mags left," Hernandez said.

"Three magazines of 9MM and 20 rounds left in my M4," Allen chimed in with a delated accountancy of his munitions.

The three operators curiously contemplated their crummy situation. They were low on ammo. They were low on morale. They were low on manpower. The situation was looking as dire as wet tee-shirt contest that was running out of cold water.

"Well, this is it," the First Sergeant said while grabbing the door handle to the next bio lab.

Chapter 7: The Final Countdown

"Since were both good as dead, might as well get to know each other a little better."

"Good as dead, huh? Speak for yourself Grandpa. I plan on getting the heck out of here."

The wounded Sergeant and the Mercenary shared a brief moment of levity among the sprawled-out body parts, broken beakers and collapsing building. The silence was broken by a blood curdling scream. Maddox pivoted her head and scoped out a potential 'Alamo' for the two to get situated. She found the perfect spot, a small office at the end of a long corridor. The office was at the end of an L-shaped corridor. One road led to the stairwell and the other led directly to the door of the office. She kicked in the door and hurled Mike Allen into the room.

"Let's rest up here for a moment. We can hold up in here until we figure out a solid game plan."

"A plan? Ha!", Mike Allen said while coughing up some blood. He smiled for a second and wiped off the blood from his chin. The blood was smeared across his muzzle

256

like a teenage girl putting on lipstick for the first time.

"I don't know about you Allen, I still like our odds."

"I give us 20 to 1. At best, I give us 15 to 1."

"I'll take that bet any day and twice on Sunday."

Allen snickered at her robust response.

"Why do you do it, Maddox?"

"Do what? Be a MERC?"

"Yeah…"

"Uh. The money, you big dummy. Why else would anyone do it?"

"Ah. How noble...", he said sarcastically while riling in pain.

"Look. The way I see it. We both live for our freedoms. We both fight for our freedoms. We both love our freedoms. We both will probably die for our freedoms. Why not get rich in the process?"

"Fair enough."

The Sergeant took a moment to regroup and regain his composure. He'd been shot before, it wasn't the most enjoyable experience, but he knew how to control the decline. He slowed his breathing and checked his wounds. His brief assessment was positive. The 'quick-clot' had stopped the bleeding and the lacerations weren't as deep as he initially thought.

"I heard stories about Al "Mad dog" Maddox…"

"Yeah? Any of them good?"

"No, not really."

"Then, they're probably all accurate," she replied and chuckled.

"You weren't exactly what I was picturing, Al."

"It's short for Alessandra."

"Ah, that makes sense."

"If it's any consolation. You weren't exactly what I was expecting either."

"Really?"

"Yeah. You Recon guys sure do bitch a lot when you take a bullet. It's a through and through, get over it. Stop being such a girly-man," she said with a wince of heartfelt words. If humor was the best medicine, she dashed a pinch of it on every sentence. It worked wonders on the Sergeant's attitude. His spirits had a renewed vigor. Was it enough to fight his way out of the facility? Time would tell.

"Alessandra is a strong name."

"I'm a strong woman."

"Undoubtedly so. Do you know the etymology of your name?"

The Mercenary looked over at Mike Allen with a confused gaze. She answered the Sergeant by shrugging her shoulders in a perplexed manner.

"All I know is that it's Italian."

"Alessandra means, "the Protector of Men"."

"How fitting?"

"Indeed…"

259

CLACK. CLACK. CLACK.

A burst of gunfire rang out down the hallway. The two simultaneously drew what little strength was left and aimed their firearms at the closed door. Their bodies ached in pain and neither one of the combatants was able to steady their weapon. The Sergeant's hand trembled with every passing second. The sidearm weighed heavily on the Sergeant's hand. He grabbed onto the bottom of the receiver in hopes to recover his stability. The mercenary hardly noticed Sergeant Allen fumbling around with his weapon. She was trained on the door, like a Doberman Pincher looking at a full dinner bowl.

"Take a breath Sergeant. I think we're fine, for now."

Sergeant Allen clasped onto Lindell's pocket bible; it was the one memento he reclaimed from his fallen team members. The pages were almost illegible due to the blood stains. He flipped through the pages for something to read and stumbled onto one of the bookmarked pages.

It read, *"I am the resurrection and the life. The one who believes in me will live, even though they die; and whoever lives by believing in me will never die. Do you believe this?"*

Maddox walked over to Sergeant Allen and grabbed the bible from his hand. She slammed the passage closed in a fit of rage.

"God gave up on us the second we stepped onto this island. If you want to have faith, have faith in me, like I have faith in you. We are all we got right now. It's you and me against the world. That's the only way we survive, by working together as a team," Maddox said while tucking away the bible into her back pocket.

Maddox knelt down and tucked her 45-caliber handgun into her waistband. She bowed her head and dumped the remnants of her canteen over the back of her head. The water flowed over hear head washing away the dried blood stains. The watered-down blood pooled below her feet and created a feint pinkish circle around her body. She pulled her hair back as tight as the skin over a drum. Her hands had a firm stranglehold over her outstretched hair. She rang out her hair like a soaked dish sponge ready to get squeezed. She methodically put her ballcap back on and adjusted it to her liking. The mercenary turned her head over to Mike Allen while she was

261

stuffing her ponytail into the back of her ballcap.

"What'd you say Sarge? Time for an ammo check," she said.

The Sergeant obliged with a smile. He appreciated the fact she was focused on the mission, even if she was forced into it. He grabbed his M4 and used the buttstock to push himself off the ground. Maddox flung a chair over to Sergeant Allen's position. He Instinctively grabbed the chair with his free hand. The Sergeant plopped down into the chair and began to examine the M4. It was covered in soot and blood.

"Okay. Let's see what we got," the Sergeant said.

He grabbed onto the M4 and started maneuvering his hand down to the Magazine Release Button. He took his thumb and with what little strength he could clicked down on the button. The standard pressure required to detach a magazine from an M4 assault rifle was approximately one pound of pressure, but for the Sergeant even this was a daunting task. The button produced a loud CLICK sound that reverberated across the room. The magazine dropped out of the receiver and the Sergeant managed to catch it right before it hit the floor. He held it in his hand, but to his chagrin, the magazine was empty. He looked back at the M4's charging handle, not ready for the inevitable outcome. He yanked back on the charging handle and a single round of 5.56mm popped out of the ejection port.

"Well, there you go. Not a total loss," the Sergeant said as he recovered the round and stuck it back into the empty magazine.

Maddox looked on with a little less zeal than before. Her spirits were somewhat dampened with the dire position the two now faced. She opened the cylinder of the revolver by pounding down on the cylinder release button. The six-round cylinder flung open from the revolver. The Mercenary made sure to take a soothing breath to calm her nerves. She lifted the revolver and pointed it into the air. The shell casings slowly dropped to the ground.

Cling. Clink. Cling. Clang. Clink. Clang.

The two looked down at the ground, like kids sprawling out pillow cases full of candy the day after Halloween.

To the surprise of the Mercenary, there were two unspent rounds. She quickly grabbed the rounds and intently inspected them.

"Well, we're not totally hosed," the Sergeant said.

"Hold on there skippy," she responded while further examining the 45-Caliber rounds. She slowly turned the rounds around to examine the head of the cartridge. The integrity of the rounds seemed to be fine at first glance, at least on the first round she inspected. She juggled the rounds and swapped them in her hands.

"Just our luck," she said.

Mike Allen looked over at her and asked, "Huh?"

"The firing pin slammed down on this round, but it didn't fire. We got one possible dud and one good round. Perfect," she said sarcastically.

"One for each of us. How about that?"

"Yeah, or one for each of them," she replied in an encouraging tone.

"Time for some 'get-back'? Yeah, I like the sound of

264

that," the Sergeant said in an attempt to muster some energy.

The Sergeant pulled an MRE from his backpack and started tearing it open with a disjointed zeal.

"You're kidding me, right?"

"What? You don't like freeze dried food?"

"First of all. I don't consider an MRE food. Eww. Heck no! Hold on," the Mercenary started rummaging around the office. She was looking for some hidden desk drawer snacks. The Mercenary was keen to human behavior, she figured the food on the island was probably sparing and a prudent rational scientist would horde snacks.

"Ah! Here we go," she said while grabbing onto something in an open drawer.

To Mike's surprise she pulled out some energy bars. She held them up like playing cards. As far as Mike could tell they were mana from heaven. She flung one of the bars over to him and opened the other by ripping it open with her mouth. Mike and Maddox scarfed down the energy bars, like two vacuums sucking up dust from an old carpet.

Kaboom!

Chowtime was interrupted by a sudden impact. What could only be described as a short loud explosion. The pair immediately made eye contact and attempted to assess the situation.

"What was that?"

"It sounded like it came from the reactor room."

Based on the location of the explosion, that only left one option on the table. The failsafe had activated the building began to collapse in on itself. Mike and Maddox were now operating on a severely truncated timetable. The odds of making it topside were increasingly becoming a distance memory.

"It's time to dance through the pain," she said.

"I don't know how to dance, but I do know a lot about pain. I'll take point. You cover my Six. We only have to clear two floors and we can make a break to the helipad. We jump off the fucking rooftop if we have to. Either way, we are getting the hell out of this facility. It's about time we get the hell off of plum island."

The Mercenary sprung to her feet and gently nudged open the door of the office. The door made a creaking sound that carried down the corridor of the hallway. Mike rose to his feet and put his hand on Maddox's left shoulder.

"You take the lead. I'll cover your six," the First Sergeant reluctantly recommended to Maddox.

Maddox wasn't naïve of her situation; she would have to step up and carry the Sergeant to the finish line. Maddox lacked any resemblance of a contingency plan, so Mike was her ticket off the island. She pulled D'Stefano's knife from her boot and held it in her left hand. In her right hand she held the revolver. She dove into the hallway and started making her way to the stairwell. Mike followed the Mercenary as close as he could. As she progressed down the hallway, she quickened her pace. Unknowingly to the Mercenary she began to create significant distance between the two. The Sergeant's night vision goggles were compromised in the commotion. They fizzled and flickered as he fidgeted with the settings. Maddox maneuvered her way to the

267

end of the hallway and stood ready at the entrance to the stairwell. The door to the stairwell was severely compromised, but with a little elbow grease she could probably get it open.

"You know I can't let get out of here alive…"

Maddox stumbled back from the door and pointed her revolver at it. The mercenary was barely able to control her sidearm. It was shaking like the flicker of a candle dancing in the wind. The heavy steel frame of the Colt-45 weighed heavily on the Mercenaries hand like the first time a kid picks up a bowling ball.

"Dirk…?"

"The fact you made it this far is astonishing, really," Dirk snickered from inside the stairwell.

The only thing that separated the former teammates was a 2-inch steel door. Maddox was practically foaming at the mouth to get some payback.

"Dirk, I brought you into this world. And I sure as hell can take you out of it."

"Like I said Maddox. I can't let you get of here."

268

"Why don't you open this door and find out?"

"Fine by me."

The Mercenary kicked on the Emergency Exit release for the door and it flung open towards Maddox. She instinctively hopped out of the way diving into some cover. Dirk stepped into the hallway like a conquering king returning to his castle. Dirk stood in the doorway of the stairwell with nothing more than a bayonet in his hand. His body was nearly camouflaged in bile laden blood.

"What a *fucking* day, huh?"

Click.

Maddox stood up tall and pulled back the hammer on her revolver. She pointed it at her former coworker with bad intentions. Dirk looked at her skeptically.

"What're you gonna do with that?"

"What I should have done a long time ago…", she said while placing her hand firmly on the trigger of the revolver.

Dirk dropped the bayonet and held his hands up in the air.

CLACK!

Dirk dropped to his knees with a gaping bullet hole protruding from his chest cavity. His knees hitting the floor made a loud THUD. Smoke protruded from the barrel of her gun and wafted up towards the ceiling like a couple sitting in bed post lovemaking holding dimly lit cigarettes.

"Damn… That fucking hurt," Dirk said as he looked up at Maddox.

"What-the…"

Dirk robotically lifted himself up from off the ground and dusted his uniform off. He poked the wound with his hand and a blackish blood oozed out of the wound onto his index finger.

"That's new…", he said surprised to be alive.

Dirk rushed his former colleague like a Heavy Weight Boxer blitzing his opponent. She pulled the trigger a second time.

Clack!

Maddox was overjoyed the bullet turned out not to be a dud. The second bullet ricocheted off of Dirk's forehead. His head was snapped back by the bullet. He slowly turn his head back towards Maddox. Unfortunately for Maddox it was just a grazing shot. Black blood discharged from Dirk's forehead and covered the better half of his face.

Dirk continued his assault and attempted to close the distance on Maddox. She flung her combat knife wildly as she back away from her former colleague. Her attempts were noble, yet ultimately ineffective. Every blow that she landed on the mercenary only enraged him further. Maddox was able to land a piercing blow and plunged the knife into Dirk's chest. He slumped his head over, but only for a brief moment. He grabbed on to her wrist and slammed his hand down onto it, shattering the bones in her arm. Maddox riled out in pain as she dangled down on the ground with a broken wrist. He flung the mercenary into the nearest steel wall, like a tantrum prone toddler tossing a ragdoll around on a playground.

Dirk stood in the hallway and examined the knife in his chest. He grabbed onto it with both hands and began to slowly pull it out of his chest. Just as the knife began to recede from his chest, he paused for a moment to look down at his former boss. She looked up at him with a smile. She rolled over and hopped up off the ground. Maddox unlatched her utility belt and wrapped it around her arm like a boa constrictor wrapping around a gazelle.

"I'm glad you can still smile. Not to many people enjoy the feeling of their own death," he said with a big ass knife sticking out of his chest.

"I give it as good as I get it," she replied.

Dirk noticeably slowed down with the knife protruding out of his chest. Maddox hit him directly in the heart and the effects were compounding on Dirk. She was doing the mental gymnastics in her head. She stepped to her right and Dirk stepped to his left. The two mercenaries began to encircle each other like a couple novice dancers trying to learn the *Waltz* for the first time. Maddox was in a vendetta kind of mood and decided to go for the Nuclear Option. She summersaulted forward at the Mercenary and jumped up into the air throwing a superman punch. As she sprang into the air with her hand cocked back to strike down at the knife, Dirk outstretched his arm and grabbed her by the neck. She dangled in the air like a fish out of water. Dirk watched the life precipitously drain from her body. She languished in pain. Blood seeped from her eye sockets as she hung from his death grip.

Dirk started up his lambasting dialogue once more, "I've been wanting to do this for a long time…"

Just as he was about to give his "evil bad guy" speech a sound interrupted him from behind. It was the all too familiar sound of a charging handle pulled back on an M4 assault rifle. Dirk turned his head to the direction of the sound only to be met with America's best, a uranium tipped 5.56x45mm NATO round shot from point blank range. The round traveled at 2,970 feet per second, all courtesy of First Sergeant Mike Allen.

The round blew out of the back of Dirk's skull spewing brain matter and chunks of bone across the room. It splattered the wall of the hallway like an early impressionist painting that might be hung up in some hoity toity art gallery. Mike dropped the M4 onto the floor and caught the falling mercenary as she broke free of Dirk's clutches.

Whoomb. Whoomb. Whoomb. Whoomb.

The blades of the Black Hawk helicopter had a distinctive sound like the motor on a finely tuned air conditioner. Mike and Maddox stared up at the skyline as a Black Hawk swooped down onto the roof of Building 257. Mike Allen was barely able to prop himself up, even with the assistance of Maddox at his side. She slid her hands under his armpit and tossed his arm over her shoulder, like someone posting up a scarecrow.

"Hold on old-timer. We're almost home," she said in a reassuring tone of voice.

"I'm glad you kept your sense of humor intact," the Sergeant said.

Two men burst out of the Black Hawk and surrounded the helicopter in a defensive position. The first, a familiar face to Mike Allen, to Mike's surprise it was Detachment Commander Russel. Russel pulled the cigar from his mouth and waved over to Mike Allen.

276

"Looks like our ride is here," Allen said with some encouragement.

"Looks that way," Maddox said hesitantly.

The two stumbled over to the Black Hawk like a couple of drunks getting tossed out of 'last call'. Commander Russel lowered his weapon and started walking towards their position. He tossed his cigar into the wind and shouted, "We heard an S.O.S over the Comm line. Hope we aren't too late."

Mike and Maddox stopped in their tracks and looked at each other with a comical disbelief.

"Sergeant Allen. You look like shit."

"Sir, yes sir," he replied to the Commander.

"Let's get you on this bird ASAP," the responded to his favorite son.

The Detachment Commander put his fingers in his mouth and let out a loud whistle. Luckily, the weather had tampered down enough for the other Marine to hear. The Commander pointed to Sergeant Allen and the Marine ran over to grab him from Maddox. Maddox obliged and let the Marine swoop him up out of her arms. The Marine and Allen trudged over to the Black Hawk.

"Who the hell are you?", the Detachment Commander asked Maddox.

"I'm...", the Mercenary paused to think about her answer. Sergeant Allen looked back for a moment and the two made eye contact.

"I'm..."

"She's one of the fisherman!", Allen shouted with his last ounce of strength. Before she could finish her answer, Allen interjected on her behalf. He knew that if the Commander found out the truth, she was a disposable asset and as good as dead.

The Commander looked her up and down, he wasn't sure what to make of her. He looked back at Mike Allen with a pinch of disbelief. The Commander knew quite a few fishermen in his day and well, Maddox did not seem like the typical fisherman. Instead of letting his masculine bullshit get in the way of his common sense, he only politely inquired further.

278

"Fisherman, huh? Is that so-?", he asked the Mercenary.

"Maddox is my name and fish is my game," she said with a smile and a wink.

"Uh-huh…"

"The names Alessandra Maddox. Nice to meet you," she said and outstretched her hand. There were a lot of things the Detachment Commander would never do, but shake a pretty young ladies' hand was not one of them.

He latched onto her hand and asked, "Do a lot of Fisherman know how to handle the business end of a Colt 45?"

Maddox started to blush and realized in her other hand was an empty revolver. A gun without bullets was just basically a big ass paperweight. She held the gun up slightly and looked it over. She laughed and daintily tossed it to the ground like penny down a well.

"A girls gotta know how to protect herself. It's a dangerous world out there," she said while attempting to turn up the charm.

The Detachment Commander was born at night, but not

last night. He didn't make it to the top by trusting people blindly. Unfortunately for the Commander, the ground beneath his feet was shifting.

"Given the fact this building is about to collapse, why don't we make like a tree and get the fuck out of here?", he asked the operator.

"You read my mind," she replied.

The two ducked their heads and sprinted to the chopper like a couple of bank robbers making a hasty retreat to the get-away-car. The Detachment Commander jumped up onto the Black Hawk. With a hop, skip and a jump, Maddox followed in kind.

Without hesitation the detachment Commander looked over to the Black Hawk pilot and yelled, "Son, get us the hell out of here. Pronto."

Mike Allen was propped up against the back of the cockpit. He shot the Commander a thumbs up and said, "Sounds good to me." One of the Marines aboard the Black Hawk was tending to his wounds. It was mostly simple bandage work, but due to the lift off the Marine was fumbling around with the cloth and tape. Mike was covered in duct tape and loosely held together cloth bandages, like a cheap children's Halloween costume of a Mummy.

"Sergeant, I'm going to need you to sit still while I fix your dressings," the Marine pleaded with the ailing Sergeant.

The humming of the Black Hawk deafened any attempt at cordial conversation. Luckily for the pilot the storm had subsided and the weather was somewhat tolerable. The Detachment Commander kept his gaze locked on the Mercenary.

"How's he holding up?", the Commander ask the Medical Corpsman. He turned his head on a swivel almost like an owl. He made sure to do so without breaking eye contact with the Mercenary. The Commander had a deceptive look about him, but the Mercenary was unphased and was hell bent on keeping up her little charade.

"Sir, he has dozens of minor lacerations. Breaks on both the left fibula and radius. He sustained two gunshot wounds, which were both through-and-throughs…", the

Marine spouted out casually like a waitress reading off the daily specials.

"What's your assessment?"

"He'll be fine. He's a Marine, sir."

"That's what I like to hear, son. Hoo-rah!"

The Detachment Commander pulled a cigar from out of his left pocket and rubbed it across his upper lip. He enjoyed the scent of unlit cigars, almost as much as he enjoyed the scent of lit cigars. He pulled out a zippo and flicked back the base lid from the lighter. It snapped back and made that oh-so typical sound of a zippo.

Clink!

The Commander started flickering on the flint wheel of the zippo lighter. The archaic lighter was as predictable as a broken clock, in that it was right twice a day. The Commander held on to this lighter for the better part of his military career, mostly for sentimental value. He slowly brought the flame up to the cigar and lit it up. As the flame burned the tip of the cigar, the Commander puffed down to ignite it. He flicked the Zippo lid back and stuffed it back in his pocket.

"Tell me again," he said with a big cigar shoved into his mouth. The cigar pushed his left cheek to the side creating a large bulge of skin like someone who stuck a jawbreaker into their mouth.

"Sorry?", the Mercenary was genuinely confused by his line of inquiry.

She started nervously tapping on her knee, like a drummer tapping on a drum pedal. Unfortunately for Maddox she was completely unaware of this subtle tell. The Detachment Commander picked up on her nervousness, but didn't make much of it. As far as he could tell, these two just went through hell and back and then back again.

"Tell me again, what were you doing fishing in the middle of a storm?", he asked with a deeper tone of voice.

The Commander took his cigar out of his mouth and blew the smoke into her face. Maddox was unsure of what to make of his gesture. As far as she could tell, she was still on a good footing with the Commander. The

Commander patiently waited for an answer. He gingerly held on to the cigar, placing it between his index and middle finger.

"Oh, it's a long story," she said dismissively to downplay the reality of the situation.

"I'm sure. But, why don't you humor me? We have a long ride back to base camp," he said.

"Ah. Well, what can I say? We fucked up, royally," she said.

"Clearly," he said and scoffed at her terse remark.

The two shared a smile and a moment to revel in laughter. The Mercenary was soaked in blood and smelt like spent shell casings. She reeked of death like a two-week-old pile of garbage.

"Are you injured?", the Commander asked somewhat confused by her almost unblemished appearance. He was unsure how his best operator barely scraped by, while a mere fisherman was virtually unscathed.

"I'm fine," the Mercenary said while attempting to conceal her many wounds.

"Let me have the Medical Corpsman come over and check you out. It's the least we can do,"

"Well, if you insist. Thanks,"

The Commander put his fingers in his mouth and let out another loud whistle. He was happy as a pig in shit with that cigar. The Commander started tapping on the handle of his M9 sidearm. Maddox wouldn't have paid it much attention, except it made a loud clang every time his pinky ring tapped onto the steel handgun.

"Come take a look at our esteemed guest," the Commander said to the Medical Corpsman. The Medic finished up with Sergeant Allen and made his way over to the Mercenary. The Corpsman walked over with his legs slightly bent and hunched over like a crab.

Whoomb. Whoomb. Whoomb. Whoomb.

The Mercenary timed the humming of the blades to help calm her nerves. She could see the mainland on the horizon and was becoming more hopeful of her situation.

"Let me take a look at you. Where does it hurt?", he

asked the Mercenary.

"Believe it or not, I'm actually feeling pretty damn good."

"Uh-huh," the Marine said with some healthy skepticism. The Marine began to examine the Mercenary's body in great detail.

"How does she look?", the Commander asked the Marine.

"Let me take a look at some of these bandages and I'll let you know," he responded.

The Marine grabbed her arm bandage and started to unwrap it. The Mercenary had begun to space out and detached herself from the situation like an employee counting down the last 15 minutes of work. The Medical Corpsman delicately removed the bloodied bandage from her right arm. Layer after layer came off from her arm, like leaf's falling from a tree in the middle of fall. The Marine finally made it to the bottom of the bandages like a dog digging up a bone.

"What the hell?"

The Detachment Commander looked over to the Medical Corpsman for some kind of insight. He peered over to see what all the fuss was about. Maddox broke her trance for a second and looked down at her arm. To her surprise, her arm was baron. There wasn't so much as a soft-tissue scar left from the knife wound.

"What the fuck indeed," the Commander said.

The Detachment Commander wasn't exactly sure what they both were talking about, so he pulled the Medical Corpsman aside for an off-the-books conversation. They pulled in close to Mike Allen and asked, "What the hell happened in there, son?"

Mike started puckering his lips like a newborn baby showing signs of hunger. The Detachment Commander noticed and snapped his fingers in the direction of the Medical Corpsman.

"Marine, get the Sergeant some water."

The Medical Corpsman pulled his canteen from his backpack. The Corpsman outstretched his arm and offered the canteen to the Sergeant. The water in the canteen swashed and shook, like a hightide splashing

287

against the shoreline. The turbulence had kicked up again. The arm of the Corpsman started to shiver as he held out the canteen to the Sergeant. Mike snatched the canteen from the Marines hand like a fireman clamping onto an out-of-control fire hose. He quickly popped the lid off and began to pour the bottle all over his face, like someone looking up while standing under a waterfall shower for the first time. The Sergeant emptied the contents of the canteen and impulsively threw it out of the helicopter.

"Your friend over there looks pretty unscathed," the Medical Corpsman said while pointing back to the Mercenary with his thumb over his shoulder.

The Sergeant's view of the Mercenary was obstructed by the Commander and the Marine. He was getting a suspicious feeling that was intentionally coordinated. It was a by-the-books interrogation tactic.

"Unscathed? What're you kidding me? You pulling my leg or something?", the Sergeant asked in a baffled tone of voice.

The Commander placed his hand on Mike's shoulder

and asked, "What'd did you find down there, son?"

"What did we find?"

"What happened?"

"We stumbled across a virus…"

"Was it SSS-1?", the Commander asked abruptly and without hesitation.

The Sergeant took a second to absorb the Commander's almost accusatory line of questioning. The Commander's knowledge of SSS-1 piqued Mike Allen into heightened state of awareness. The Sergeant started looking around the Black Hawk for some kind of clue. He made an attempt to get up, which was molested by the Medical Corpsman. Presumably, he wasn't in a condition to get up. His mind was willing, but his body was unable. Mike inconspicuously looked back towards the cockpit. The compass showed a northern orientation, which was rather peculiar to the Sergeant. Especially considering the base would be west of the island.

"Affirmative, sir," he responded.

The Sergeant sought it best to keep his answers terse and

on point. The Commander and the Medical Corpsman shared an incredulous glance. Without a word spoken, the Commander and the Marine were speaking loud and clear. The Marine clicked the safety off from his M4 and switched it to automatic fire mode. The Commander slowly slid his hand down his waist to his holster. He judicially went to grab his M9, but was met with nothing. His holster was as empty as a box of condoms on prom night.

Click!

The Commander's face turned pale white as he heard the familiar sound of an M9 cocked back ready to fire. The life drained from his face and what remained was pure apprehension.

"Drop your weapon," the Mercenary said to the Medical Corpsman.

The Medical Corpsman had little experience in close quarters combat and looked over to the Commander for some kind of guidance. Neither man was eager to get shot in the back. The Commander turned his head back to glance at the 'fisherman' and figure out an amicable solution to this lopsided standoff. She quickly pointed the gun out of the Black Hawk and fired a single waring shot into the air.

"Marine, toss your weapon aside. The next shot goes into your ass," she screamed.

The Commander motioned over to the Marine and said, "It's okay, son. Toss it."

The Maine obliged and unslung his rifle. He methodically took the weapon and shoved it to the side.

"Gentlemen, I really appreciate the ride. But, this is where I get off," the Mercenary said with a visceral smile.

Her veins began to profusely pulsate. Her forearms began to belligerently bulge. Her neck muscles began to uncontrollably ungulate. The Mercenary began to peer over the open cargo cabin door. The helicopter was traveling around 200 MPH and hovering approximately 1000-feet above the Sea level. The Mercenary started removing the remainder of her bandages like a tourist in Seattle removing excess layers of clothing.

"Oh, wow! This shit really works," she said with some amazement.

Mike Allen instinctively knew she was infected, but couldn't figure out how it happened. He was trying to piece it together, but just couldn't line up when it happened. The Mercenary could see the wheels turning in his head and said, "Mike, don't feel bad. I wasn't being completely honest with you. When you found me, I was already very much infected."

"What're you saying?"

The Mercenary beamed bright smile at the First Sergeant. She found a sick sense of enjoyment in his pending revelation.

"Dirk wasn't trying to stop you. It was you, all along. He was trying to stop you from getting out," the Sergeant said.

The Mercenary holstered her newly acquired sidearm in her waistband. She started slowly applauding the Sergeant's epiphany.

Clap. Clap... Clap. Clap.

"Bingo! You got it! I take back what I said about you RECON guys."

The Commander looked back and retrained his focus on the Sergeant. Clearly, the Sergeant had some explaining to do. The Sergeant bowed his head in shame, the gig was up. He looked like a kid about to be placed in timeout.

"I'd love to stay and chat boys, but I gotta run. Time is money after all," she said while unholstering the *M9*.

She pointed the M9 square at the Detachment Commander. The Detachment Commander didn't so much as flinch. He hunkered down and took a long puff of his cigar.

"You're one tough hombre, huh?", she asked the Commander.

The Commander was unphased by her threatening gesture and belittling question. The way he figured it, if she wanted to kill him, she would have done it already.

"Sweety. If you think this is the first time someone shoved a gun in my face, you're sorely mistaken."

"That's fair," she said while snatching the cigar from the Commander.

Maddox pressed on the mag release button and caught the falling magazine with her left hand. She tossed it out the window without a moment's hesitation. She pulled back on the slide of the M9 releasing the chambered round. The gun was dry, so she tossed it back to the Commander. The Commander instinctively tried to catch the M9 and fumbled it to the ground. Just as he was about to pull a fresh magazine Maddox jumped from the helicopter. He slammed the magazine into the receiver and started firing wildly into the air.

Clack. Clack. Clack. Clack.

The sounds of gunshots were murmured by the humming of the Black Hawk blades. The Commander unloaded his entire magazine out in the general direction of the plummeting mercenary. He had about as good of chance hitting her as a kid playing one of those carnival claw machines grabbing at a stuffed animal. The Commander fired off all of his rounds and the slide of the M9 opened to let him know it was empty. He uncontrollably kept pulling back on the trigger and in a fit of rage threw his

M9 out of the helicopter.

"Barkeep! Another round for my new friend over here," the man said and slammed his palm on the countertop.

The smacking sound made a reverberating god smack that rang across the semi-uninhabited bar. The bartender perused his vast bourbon offering. The bottles came in a colorful array of reds, browns and burgundies. The bartender poured over the labels of bourbon and arrived at the cheapest one of the bunch. The bottle stuck out like a sore thumb. It had a hand written label over a piece of duct tape, which read, "House Bourbon".

"Ah. There *you* are," the bartender said while seizing his favorite bottom shelf bourbon.

The bartender snagged the bottle from the bourbon rack. He stood across from the Sergeant and carefully poured another shot of bourbon into the Sergeant's sipping glass. The Sergeant found it rather ironic, calling it a sipping glass. Was that supposed to make him feel like less of an alcoholic? The Sergeant stared at the glass with a melancholic expression. He picked it up and swirled it around for a while. The bourbon made these large concentric circles as it swirled in the glass. The bourbon had the faded hue of what surmounted to overpriced watered-down soda with a splash of alcohol.

"So... then what happened?", the mysterious stranger asked former First Sergeant Mike Allen.

Mike slugged back the drink and firmly slammed the glass down on the bar top. The bottom of the hard glass made a loud, "*Thud!*" No one in the bar batted an eye or so much as flinched a muscle. People at this place tended to keep to themselves, which is the main reason why Mike frequented this bar so often. The bar top was one of those modern countertops only relegated to upscale D.C. social clubs. He was frustrated by the fervor of the man fawning over his fantastical story. He knew it was hard to believe, that's why he was so forthcoming. Mike didn't see much utility in varnishing a story nobody would believe. The bar couched itself as a 'Social Club', which was one step removed from a Gentleman's bar or something you'd find in a Mafia movie. For D.C. standards, this place was kind of a dive bar. The bar top was about thirty feet long and made of a faded fake off-white marble.

"What is this, twenty questions?", Mike snapped back at the man and shoved his glass back to the bartender.

The bartender took no offense to his rude off-the-cuff gesture. Liquor tended to suspend formal platitudes and relinquished most people of normative pleasantries. He snatched the glass off the countertop and secured it under the spout of the bourbon. The bartender clearly took a lot of pride is his free pour. Bourbon flowed out of the bottle like tears falling from heaven.

"Oh, no, no, no. Sorry to be so intrusive. I'm just captivated by your story. That's all," the man said slightly defensively.

Mike clasped back onto the glass of bourbon and began to sulk over his drink. His companion started twirling his martini glass to mirror Mike's behavior. When he picked his glass up from the bar he noticed a slight ring of condensation forming on the countertop. The man slid over a complementary coaster for Mike to put under his glass. He thanked the man by casually continuing the conversation.

"What happened? I'll tell you what happened. The

building ended up collapsing in on itself, like one of those seaside condo complex demolitions you'd see on cable TV. Instead of rebuilding, the government just decided to cover it all up, literally. They poured hundreds of tons of concrete over the site and just buried it," he explained.

Mike started tapping on the brim of his Bourbon glass as if he was lost in deep contemplation over the entire situation. He was clearly grappling with the reality of what he endured. He was clearly pondering the entire journey. He was clearly lost in deep thought over his conundrum. This whole exercise was rather cathartic for Mike, but he struggled retelling all the key details of the story. The way Mike figured it, if the Military brass was able to bury the story, then why couldn't Mike?

"Mmm... Sounds like a real cluster fuck."

"You don't know the half of it, buddy. I was stuck between a rock and hard place. The brass wanted to sweep this whole thing under the rug. So, they granted me a Medical Discharge and kicked me to the curb."

"All things being considered. Could've been worse?

Eh?"

"That's the understatement of the century. Could have been a lot worse. In retrospect, a lot worse. I could be rotting away in a cell at Fort Leavenworth."

"Hey, I hear the breakfast is pretty decent at 'Hotel' Leavenworth. Tuesday they do *Silver Dollar Pancakes…*"

Mike shut up for a second to think carefully about his next words. He chose them about as carefully as a newlywed couple buying their first home. The man's statement left a bad taste in his mouth, but Mike wasn't ruling out the bourbon amplifying the descent of the conversation.

"I think the risk of any of this going down in public records wasn't a risk the brass wanted to take. All it would take is some over-eager reporter, or a potential Senate hearing to make a mess of everything. God forbid someone filed a FOIA request. It was easier to discredit me and throw me to the wind."

"Mhm," the man affirmed while sipping on his room temperature Appletini.

300

"It all sounds rather fantastical. Mercenaries and Super Solider Serum. Might even make a good book."

"Right? Who would believe me? Oh, yeah, some unarmed Mercenary group was dumb enough to infiltrate a bio weapons lab on an island, right?"

"In the middle of a hurricane, no less. Yeah, who'd be that dumb? C'mon, man," the man asked.

Mike was unsure what to make of this guy. For the time being, he was making a great sounding board and freed up his bar tab.

"Yeah, who would be that dumb? Who, indeed?", Mike responded while pointing both of his thumbs back at him.

Mike turned his back to the bartender and leaned up against the bar top. He started sipping his glass while scouting out the room for some 'warm' company. He noticed that the room was unusually quiet, even for 8:00 PM it was quiet. Mike chalked it all up to his drunken paranoia and low-grade bourbon.

"So… what happened to the Mercenary?"

"Maddox?"

"Yeah, Maddox," the man said curiously.

"The Coast Guard launched a large-scale manhunt. The biggest in Naval history."

"Yeah? How'd they cover that up?"

"It was dubbed a 'joint training exercise' between local law enforcement, the Coast Guard and the Navy."

"Impressive…"

"Undoubtedly."

"So…"

"So? So, what?"

"So, did they end up finding her?"

"She jumped out of a Black Hawk with no parachute, which was traveling somewhere in the ballpark of Two-Hundred miles per hour. What do you think they found?"

"Fair enough," he replied.

"I mean, shit. Even if, somehow, she managed to survive the fall into the ocean. And, that is a big *if*."

"Big if," he interjected.

"If she somehow managed to swim to shore? During a hurricane? With no thermal gear on? I don't think so."

"You know what I think?"

"No, not really. Can't say that I do."

"I think you're a severely undervalued asset, my friend."

"Really?"

"Really, really," he said while finishing his martini.

"Well, I'd love to sit here and chat. But, I've got to get back to work," the man said.

"What is it that you do, exactly?"

Instead of an instant retort the man produced a menacing smile. It's clear that Mike's story was making an indelible impression on the man. Mike figured he was some kind of military groupie, the kind that lived vicariously through extracting stories out of veterans one

303

drink at a time.

"What do I do? What do I do... That's an interesting question Mike. I... Well, I'm an investment analyst of sorts. I find value where others do not."

"Oh. Like a stock broker or something?"

"Something like that..."

A large man in a black suit leaned over to the man and surreptitiously whispered something in his ear. The way Mike figured it, the free drinks were about to end. Mike held up his glass as a demonstrative form of gratitude, like a best man holding up a glass for a toast. At the same time, Mike realized he was spilling his guts to a complete stranger. This guy was a total stranger, and that was something Mike had to solve.

"I didn't catch your name, friend..."

The man smiled ear to ear and slid his business card over to Mike Allen. Mike didn't bother looking at it immediately. He was still rather focused on his caramel-colored drink. At this point the ice cubes had melted and watered down any remaining alcohol.

"That's because I didn't give it, friend…", he replied back to the now defunct former operator.

Mike slugged the remainder of his drink and slammed the glass on the countertop. He snagged the business card off the countertop with his left hand and a handful of bar nuts with his right.

"The name, the name is Billy. My friends call me Billy the kid," he said with a shit eating grin stained across his cheeks.

Mike looked back at Billy and then looked down at his business card. He held the business card in his hand and tapped it against the bar top.

"If you ever need work. I'm always looking for good people. Stay in touch, Mike Allen."

The End